Susanna's Christmas Wish

JERRY S. EICHER

HARVEST HOUSE PUBLISHERS
EUGENE, OREGON

All Scripture quotations are from the King James Version of the Bible.

All poetry in this book was written by Jerry Eicher, © 2012.

Cover photos © Chris Garborg; Bigstock / Robin Mackenzie, jlgoodyear

Cover by Garborg Design Works, Savage, Minnesota

SUSANNA'S CHRISTMAS WISH
Copyright © 2012 by Jerry S. Eicher
Published by Harvest House Publishers
Eugene, Oregon 97402

ISBN 978-1-62090-841-9

Printed in the United States of America

This book is dedicated to the other side of the story:
To all the Amish girls who have been left behind, to their
love, and to their life built from the ashes of what was lost.

Acknowledgments

I was more the scribe than the writer on this one. This story appeared with only the minimum of digging on my part. And thanks to the editors at Harvest House, Nick Harrison and Barb Gordon. They touched the story with great tenderness, adding beauty and grace.

One

Susanna Wagler stood by the living room window watching Herman's broad shoulders as he guided the team of horses into the field. Was he really her husband? The thought raced through her mind, and she pushed it away. These were not the thoughts a woman of God should have. Of course Herman was her husband. They had said the marriage vows in front of Bishop Jacob not three weeks ago. She could still hear Bishop Jacob's voice intoning, "Do you, sister Susanna, believe *Da Hah* has given our brother Herman to you as your husband?"

The words had hung in the air only for a moment before she whispered, "*Yah.*"

Herman was the husband *Da Hah* meant for her. She had been certain of it. As certain as she could be. He was a man deeply loved by the community for his honest ways, his open face, and his dedication to the faith of the fathers. This was why she had said *yah* to Herman's first timid request when he'd asked her home from the hymn singing. And so far Herman Wagler hadn't let her down. Not like someone else had... Susanna also pushed that thought away.

She had forgotten about him—shut his memory from her mind. But even now she shouldn't think badly of Matthew Yoder, though he had broken her heart. The truth had come out, and it was better this way. How awful would it have been if the truth had waited to appear after they were married? That was what her sister Mary told her, and she was right. Mary was wise about Matthew, having married his brother Ernest. Even before Matthew had left, Mary had seemed unsure of his intent. Older sisters were good for something after all, it seemed.

Still, Susanna tried to give Matthew the benefit of the doubt. He must have had his reasons for leaving the community. Even though she couldn't understand them…or follow him into the *Englisha* world. And his reasons were obviously greater than his love for her. That was what hurt the most when he'd informed her he didn't plan to stay in the Amish community. He hadn't been able to tell her before, he'd said, though he'd assured her he hadn't been playing her along all those years.

But a man didn't suddenly make up his mind to leave, she figured. Such a desire had to have been there for a long time. Matthew had known something, regardless of how much he insisted he hadn't. If she had loved him enough, she would have gone with him, she supposed. But how could a woman love a man who loved the *Englisha* world more than he loved her? Still, she had wavered for weeks over the matter. Struggled with the agony of it. Was she at fault? Did love require the sacrifice of everything…of all she held dear? Things like this land of her people? These open fields she'd grown up in? This place where she'd been born?

Matthew seemed to have no problem leaving all of it, and he'd soon put his words into action, getting himself placed in the *bann* in the process. As if she could face something like that. The cutting off of all contact with her past. This couldn't be love, she'd finally told herself. She could not choose this.

So Matthew was gone.

And slowly she had put the fragments of her heart back together. Finding a piece here and a piece there that fit. Herman, with his tenderness, had helped. And her heart had healed somewhat, hadn't it? She wouldn't have married Herman if it hadn't, would she?

She loved Herman. She did. Herman was the kindest man around. She should be thankful he had even considered her. Especially after Matthew left and caused such a stir in the community. No Amish young man would have been blamed for avoiding her completely, like she was a second-rate, cast-off shirt. And yet Herman hadn't thrown her away. He had asked her home from the hymn singing and eventually asked if she would be his *frau*. Someone to love and cherish forever while they lived on this earth. Herman had done that, and was that not love?

Susanna's eyes lingered on Herman's face as he turned the team of horses around. The prancing hooves left tracks in the light dusting of the overnight snow. For a moment Herman glanced toward the house, and she ducked behind the drapes. It wouldn't be decent for him to see her staring at him from the window. Not yet. Even if he was her husband. They should learn to know each other better first.

When Susanna stole another look, Herman was headed out over the open fields, hanging on to the lines. He is a handsome man, she told herself. And one she was thankful to have as her husband.

There was at least one brokenhearted girl in the community that she knew of. Herman had left behind Ruth Byler. She sure hadn't kept her desires to have Herman take her home from the hymn singing a secret. And if there was one who did so openly, there had to be others who had hid their feelings. Yet Herman had chosen her.

Susanna turned back to the kitchen with a sigh. This had to stop. This wondering and puzzling over things. She had expected it would be over after the wedding. In fact, there had been plenty of signs during the weeks before the wedding that her doubts had flown away. Now they apparently were back in force.

But they would live through this, Susanna told herself. Herman loved her and she loved him. He had made that plain enough in the days since the wedding. And she had no reason to complain. She was sure Herman was aware that her heart hadn't totally healed from Matthew, but he was being kind and understanding. What woman wouldn't love such a man?

Susanna ran hot water into the kitchen sink while she brought the last of the breakfast dishes to the counter. Herman's plate was sopped clean—it looked almost washed, like it always did. Even though it had been a large breakfast of eggs, bacon, and home fries she'd fixed him. Herman would have made a *gut* bachelor, that was for sure. The way he kept everything tidy around himself. And yet he felt the need of her, felt it necessary to bring her into his life.

But why?

Because he loved her, of course, Susanna told herself. There didn't need to be a reason beyond that. Perhaps it was the conversation at the breakfast table this morning that was bringing this indecision up again. Well, it was more of an argument, really. Their first timid disagreement. And she had been shocked at the feelings that rose up inside of her. The insistence that Herman see things her way. And she had even grown angry, though Herman hadn't, even as he remained firm. There would be no celebration of Christmas in their new home. And they wouldn't be going to her parents' place to celebrate either. It was not the way of his family, and it would not be their way.

Susanna washed the dishes and stared out the window at the snow. Soon the snow would be falling in earnest, the flakes floating past this very window. The joy and hope of Christmas would be in the air. The celebration of the Christ child in the manger would be coming. Was this feeling just an *Englisha* thing, like Herman claimed? He said her family had given in to worldly influences and his family had not.

Yet how could this be true? Her family didn't celebrate Christmas like the *Englisha* did, with their Christmas trees and lots of store-bought presents. *Nee,* their celebration was simple. They began by gathering on Christmas morning for breakfast. In his deep voice, *Daett* would read the story of the Christ child's birth. Then the day would be spent together visiting, eating candy and goodies galore, and letting the children race around the house. Maybe that was a little like the *Englisha,* but she would be willing to adjust something, like leaving early, if that helped Herman get used to her family's ways.

But Herman had said no. No hesitation, right out, flat no.

And she had gotten angry. Even her cheeks flushed and her fingers tingled. She had stood up from the table to get a drink at the sink even though her glass was still full of water. His eyes had followed her as he seemed to be waiting for harsh words from her.

But she had not spoken them. She knew that Herman, being her husband, was in the right. And she knew what he would say further on the matter—that she knew *before* the wedding what his feelings were. He had made no secret of them. And there had been the talk with his *mamm.* Herman's *mamm* had made two or three special trips to the Keim farm before the wedding to visit Susanna. From that first visit, it seemed as if his *mamm* was sizing her up as a daughter-in-law. Would she be good enough for her Herman? That was her purpose in that first visit. She must have passed the test because there had been the second visit. That's when Mrs. Wagler told Susanna what Herman's favorite dishes were and how important it was to honor their family traditions. That was when she mentioned their longstanding abhorrence of the celebration of Christmas that had somehow infiltrated the community. Those visits had been uncomfortable enough, but then only two days after the wedding Herman's *mamm* had showed up to help her organize her kitchen. Hadn't it occurred to her that if Susanna needed such help she would have asked her own *mamm?*

Nee, she couldn't say she didn't know how Herman and his family felt about Christmas, Susanna acknowledged. And now with their first Christmas together approaching, Susanna was realizing it would also be her first Christmas without the joy she had experienced at home. *Nee*, she would never get to be at *Mamm* and *Daett's* for Christmas morning again.

Knowing about his objections beforehand wasn't making it any easier, no matter how often she'd told herself it should be. She had thought maybe there was some sort of compromise possible. Surely there had to be. Susanna sighed. It was useless, really. She already knew that. Hermann was handsome and nice and calm, but he was "Amish stubborn." That was just how it was. And she was his *frau*.

Well, she could imagine that Christmas was no big deal. Perhaps she was being silly about such a small matter. They would find something else to do on Christmas morning.

Susanna dried the plates and placed them in the cupboard above her. She would have to learn submission, that was the only answer. This was the first big test being placed before her by *Da Hah*, and she would have to pass somehow. Oh, if she only could. Who would have thought she would have trouble with being a *gut frau?* That had been the least of her expectations. A sloppy housekeeper, perhaps, or being unable to keep up with the sewing once she had a bunch of *kiener*. Those things had worried her, but letting her husband have his way about Christmas had not been on her list.

Susanna closed the cupboard door. She would learn this lesson by Christmas morning. She still had time. Thanksgiving was this week, and that left nearly a month until Christmas. Yes, that's what she would do. She would set her whole heart to the task. This would be her gift of love to Herman. She would learn to keep her mouth shut, and even if she didn't succeed right away, it would happen. She would apologize until it did happen. Surely by Christmas the task would be done. Herman would see on that morning how much progress she'd made in fitting herself into his family's lifestyle.

By Christmas Day she would love him fully, with all of her heart. What better wish to aim for than to live in total harmony with your husband, she decided. And love would keep growing in her heart for him. Perhaps not exactly the love she used to feel for Matthew, but a better love. A higher love. One that would grow from suffering.

Hadn't Matthew shown her how shallow their love used to be? He'd sure been able to cast it off as if it didn't matter.

Running to the window again, Susanna peeked out. Herman was a dim figure now, almost lost from view in the distant field. He looked intent on his work, his head bent toward the ground as his plow turned up the black dirt. Susanna turned away. How like plowing her plan was. Turning her old life under like Herman was doing to the ground today. Preparing for the spring when things come alive again. She would do the same. Plow under her selfish desires to plant a future spiritual harvest. Here was the sign as to what she should do as plain as day and right before her eyes. How like *Da Hah* to show her so quickly that He liked her plan. He would surely be answering her wish soon.

Two

*T*wo hours later Susanna finished her kitchen chores. It was a few minutes before eleven o'clock, and Susanna made her way to the barn, hoping Herman wouldn't notice. *Nee*, he was in the far corner of the field now and wouldn't see her go. Not that he would object to her going to visit her sister. In fact, he already knew she was going. But if he saw her before she had Bruce hitched to the buggy, Herman might feel compelled to leave his horses and come in to give her a hand. Especially after their argument this morning.

She knew him well enough to have that figured out. Herman would want to show her that he held nothing against her even as he stood his ground. It was better that she harness Bruce on her own. Once he saw her on the road, Herman would remember she was going to Mary's house for the day to help prepare for Thanksgiving.

Tonight she would make things up to Herman by putting a *gut* supper on the table. She had already made an overture by laying cold cuts out for his lunch. Maybe her kindness after their disagreement would cause him to consider a little about how she was feeling. It wouldn't hurt him. And by Christmastime, *Da Hah* would have worked a *gut* miracle in her, and she would have moved a long way toward being a submissive wife.

Herman's horse greeted her with a loud whinny when she walked into the barn. Already Bruce knew her well, and he apparently liked her. No doubt in part because every time Herman had called for her at her parents' place, she'd always taken the time to stroke his neck and talk to him while Herman tied him up by the barn.

"How you doing there, old man?" Susanna asked, opening the stall door to grab his halter. He bobbed his head as she ran her fingers through his mane.

"Herman put you in here for me, didn't he?" Susan looked around for a moment. "Well, I'm sorry you had to stand all morning in a tight little stall when you could have been running around the pasture. But see, my husband is trying to be nice since we had a little tiff this morning. Do you think you can understand that?"

Bruce whinnied again as she led him outside the stall to throw on the harness. With the straps on tight, he followed her willingly to the buggy and swung under the shafts when she held them up.

Bruce was a well-behaved horse, just like his owner. Steady and always helpful, though he didn't have much speed—except for short spurts downhill. But he could be counted on to get her somewhere in time and with little hassle.

"Get-up," Susanna said once she was inside the buggy and had taken up the reins. She turned to take one last look toward the back field, as they drove out the lane. Herman had spotted her now, and he was craning his neck in her direction.

Susanna leaned out of the buggy to wave, and Herman's hand came up in return. He was too far away for her to see if a smile crept across his face, but it would be there. She also knew that characteristic. He would get the message that she wasn't going to throw another fit about this morning. He would understand she had to have time to work through her feelings. In that way, he also had her figured out, which was a nice, warm thought. Herman was a patient man. They would make a *gut* couple by the time all was said and done.

Susanna slapped the reins against Bruce's back, urging him on.

As they drew close to Bishop Jacob's place, she saw a team of Belgians in the field. The bishop was also busy at fall plowing. She waved as she went past, and Bishop Jacob turned to wave back, his face breaking into a broad smile.

For Bishop Jacob to be behind the plow must mean his son-in-law must be behind on his own plowing, Susanna figured. The bishop only helped with the chores now that he'd turned his farm over to his youngest daughter's husband. They'd been married a few years now.

What would Bishop Jacob think if he knew about her little argument with Herman this morning? He probably wouldn't be smiling. But maybe he would understand that all young married couples have issues to work through. Most of those problems surely didn't involve things like celebrating Christmas or having an ex-boyfriend who was in the *bann* though.

Bishop Jacob wouldn't be holding Matthew against her, would he? He hadn't mentioned it when she and Herman had gone to ask if he would marry them. But if Bishop Jacob knew she was thinking again of Matthew, he might have something to say about it. His face would no doubt fall in disappointment. His high hopes in the young couple he had married only a few weeks ago would be troubled.

She knew Bishop Jacob had high hopes because he'd said so when she and Herman had arrived that Saturday evening to announce their wedding plans.

"*Gut* evening," Bishop Jacob had greeted them with a twinkle in his eye. This was obviously a routine he had seen many times before. "May I do anything for you?" he had asked, as if he didn't have a clue.

Herman hadn't missed a beat. Almost as if he had done this a hundred times before, he'd said, "May we have a few words with you inside?"

"Of course," Bishop Jacob had said, opening the door wide.

Once they were all settled, Herman had wasted no time. "Susanna and I have agreed to wed. And we would like to be published in two weeks—if you have no objections."

"Me? Have objections?" Bishop Jacob had laughed. "I'm expecting I'll have no objections. After I've asked the few usual questions, of course. I've been observing your courtship, and I think both of you are making a very wise choice."

Susanna had looked away from the bishop's gaze that night. She still remembered how she'd felt though—all warm inside at his kind words. How *gut* it was to know she had been doing the right thing by dating Herman and agreeing to wed him. And she still felt that way. It was just that Herman and she were having a little trouble right now. But that would all be over soon, if *Da Hah* willed it. And surely He did.

Ahead of her, Mary's house appeared, and Susanna pulled back on the reins. Bruce turned down the driveway like he knew exactly where she was going, coming to a stop at the hitching post beside the barn.

Susanna jumped down and unhitched. With a glance around, she stopped short, her hands on Bruce's halter. Why was there an *Englisha* car parked behind the barn? Beside her, Bruce lunged forward, almost stepping on her as he came out of the shafts.

"Whoa, boy!" she muttered. "I wasn't quite ready for that."

Recovering, she led Bruce toward the barn. Mary would have an explanation once she arrived at the house. An *Englisha* car behind the barn would be hard to explain though. Any *Englisha* people who stopped in, whether they were buying produce from Mary's garden or had business with her husband, Ernest, would park in plain sight.

"Howdy there," Mary's voice hollered from the front porch, jerking Susanna out of her thoughts.

"Hi," Susanna called back. "I'm taking Bruce into the barn."

"Do you need help?" Mary asked. "Ernest isn't here right now."

"Of course not!" Susanna hollered back with a laugh.

Now why would Mary ask such a thing? Mary knew she was perfectly capable of unharnessing a horse by herself. She must be in a teasing mood. But Mary wasn't exactly a teaser. Well then, she must be in a *gut* mood with Thanksgiving coming up later this week. Getting ready for family gatherings always puts *my* family members in a *gut* mood, Susanna thought. She slid open the barn door. At least Herman hadn't objected to Thanksgiving meals with her family. "If they aren't too extravagant," he'd said last year. And as long as no one ate too much. He had come to Thanksgiving last year and was apparently satisfied. Why else would he have agreed to their coming to Mary's house this year, as well as her helping Mary prepare beforehand?

If her family thought her new husband strange, they had yet to mention anything. Of course, they hadn't gone through an actual Christmas as a married couple yet. Perhaps that would make a difference.

It'll be okay, Susanna told herself, turning Bruce loose in an empty stall. She threw him a slab of hay before leaving. He was munching away when Susanna glanced over her shoulder to check on him before closing the barn door.

Mary was waiting on the front porch when Susanna stepped outside. She looked very troubled now. Had Mary also had an argument with her husband this morning? Was that it? But that couldn't be. Mary and Ernest had been together for years now, and they had doubtlessly worked through all their marriage problems.

"*Gut* morning," Susanna greeted Mary. "Is everything okay?"

"Oh, *yah*…" Mary's smile looked stiff. "I'm so glad you could come."

"Did you boil over something in the kitchen?" Susanna guessed. Mary wasn't beyond forgetting a kettle cooking on the stove.

"Oh no," Mary said, her eyes shifting toward the barn. "It's been going well all morning."

Susanna turned to look again, remembering the *Englisha* car. "Is that someone who has business with Ernest?"

Mary shook her head. "Maybe we'd better stay out here on the porch for a moment. I need to tell you something."

"What has happened?" Susanna took Mary's arm, leading her over to the rocking chairs. She sat down once Mary was seated.

Mary was breathing deeply. "I would have let you know before you came, but there was no way to get hold of you in time."

"Mary, what has happened?"

"Maybe you should just go home right now." Mary leaped to her feet. "In fact, that's what I think you should do. It would be best for everyone concerned."

Susanna pulled her sister down. "You're going to tell me right now, or I'm going to search the whole house until I find out what's wrong."

Mary's face turned white. "You shouldn't do that. I'll tell you."

Now Susanna was getting weak-kneed herself. Mary never acted like this, even when little Mose had broken his arm last summer at *Mamm* and *Daett's* place. And by the way, why were the two children not out here? Usually Mose and Laura were climbing all over her by now, happy to see her and chattering a mile a minute. All seemed too quiet.

"Mary," Susanna whispered, "tell me what's wrong."

"He came late last night," Mary whispered back. "He's inside sleeping."

"Who came?"

Now her knees really were going weak. Mary could only mean one person for her to have a reaction like this. But it couldn't be! Matthew wouldn't simply appear like this. Unannounced just before Thanksgiving. Not after leaving like he had.

"*Yah*," Mary said, as if reading her thoughts. "You're thinking right. He's stopped by for the Thanksgiving holiday. Now don't you think you'd better leave before he sees you?"

Susanna was staring at Mary. "Does he know about me? About Herman?"

Mary shook her head. "He asked about you first thing, but Ernest and I avoided his questions. I thought the children might answer him, but thankfully they weren't in the room at the time."

"He has to be told," Susanna managed to get out.

"I will—tonight. Now go home before he hears your voice."

"And leave you alone with all the Thanksgiving work?"

"There are things more important than work." Mary was on her feet, motioning down the porch steps. "Quickly, Susanna!"

Three

Susanna tried to make out what Mary was saying, but the sound wasn't registering. A thousand thoughts raced through her mind. Memories of Matthew's face as she had seen it last. Pain etched across his handsome features as he told her that he had to leave. Matthew—the man she had once loved. Matthew back at his brother's place.

How could this be? What reason would Matthew have for coming—even if it was Thanksgiving? Matthew was still in the *bann*. Why had Mary even let him in her house? "Why he is here?" Susanna asked.

Mary stopped tugging on her arm. "I don't know. He didn't say for sure—other than he's visiting over Thanksgiving. And we can't just throw Ernest's brother out of the house."

Susanna's thoughts stabbed through her. If she had married Matthew, Ernest's brother, their children would have been double cousins. She and Mary and Matthew and Ernest would forever be part of the same family. Susanna pushed the thought away. "But Matthew's in the *bann!*"

"I know that." Mary was pulling on her arm again. "Ernest and I aren't doing anything wrong. Matthew's not helping us, and he eats on the couch. You know we're not like some communities, Susanna, where they don't even talk to their fallen family members."

Susanna swallowed hard. "I want to speak with him."

"Susanna, please," Mary begged. "Not now. You're not in any condition to speak with Matthew."

Obviously her sister knew her quite well. Was her pain really that plain? Her struggles with her marriage? Had Mary seen this while she and Herman had been dating? Well, if she had, Mary could have said something. *Nee,* she was not leaving now. *Da Hah* was going to give her grace, and she was going to get over her past. "I'm not running away, Mary. He'll just come after me."

Mary looked pale, but she didn't shake her head. So she also knew, as Susanna did, that if Matthew had the nerve to show up here, he would eventually have the nerve to stop in at her place. Better to deal with him here…and now.

"Maybe you should," Mary agreed, relenting. "But somehow we have to get him out of the house soon after that."

"He's your husband's brother," Susanna said. "I guess there's not much you can do about that."

Mary was silent, her hand still on her sister's arm.

"Where are Mose and Laura?"

"Ernest took them with him. He was sharpening the blades on his plow this morning and had to run into town for supplies."

"Come then. Now is the time. Matthew will leave when he finds out I'm married. Then we can finish our day's work. We've already wasted way too much time."

Susanna led the way. This was Mary's house, but it seemed right that she was being the strong one right now. Later she could collapse and have a *gut* cry. Perhaps upstairs where Herman wouldn't walk in and hear her. Once this meeting was over, Herman need never know about it.

Inside the two women hesitated.

"What should we do?" Mary whispered. "We could start working in the kitchen, I suppose, until he shows up."

As if in answer to Mary's question, footsteps came down the stairs. Familiar footsteps, Susanna thought. How many times had she heard that light step in *Mamm* and *Daett's* house over the years when Matthew brought her home on Sunday nights?

Susanna gathered herself. Matthew had no right to be here, and she would need to be brave about this. For Mary's sake, if nothing else. And for Herman—if he ever learned about this, which hopefully he wouldn't.

A man's face, unshaven, appeared in the stair doorway. He leaned out, keeping his hands on the frame. A smile spread across his face. "I thought I heard something. So you couldn't wait to see me, could you?"

The insolence of the man! Susanna thought. How dare he? But her heart was pounding, and words refused to come out of her mouth.

Matthew looked much the same. Maybe a little older but still just as handsome—especially with that stubble on his face.

"Don't I at least get a *gut* morning?" he asked, stepping down the rest of the stairs and seating himself on the couch.

He wore a T-shirt and denim pants—with a belt. All very *Englisha* looking, but then that's what he was now.

"Susanna came over to help me," Mary spoke up at last. "We have to get started on Thanksgiving."

"You mean I don't get any breakfast? I mean, I'll eat on the couch, but I do have to eat."

"Ernest isn't here right now," Mary said. "But he'll be back before long. We'll serve lunch then."

Gut for you, Mary, Susanna thought. Standing up to Matthew like that. If the man can't get up at a decent hour like he'd been raised, let him go hungry. She'd better say something soon or Matthew would catch on to how her heart was racing. "We have to get busy," Susanna said, echoing Mary's comment.

"So…has anybody taken my place by now?" Matthew asked, his voice teasing. "Anyone bringing you home on Sunday nights?"

"Of course people have!" Mary snapped. "You knew Susanna

wasn't going to wait around like a fallen apple rotting on the ground."

"I can't say that I blame her," Matthew agreed. "So who's the lucky fellow?"

"Is that why you've come back?" Susanna faced him. "To find out what I'm doing?"

"Whoa, as feisty as ever." Matthew smiled. "Some things never do change—like most everything in the community. Kind of locked down for eternity."

"So you've come to insult us too?" Susanna glared at him.

"No," Matthew said, his smile fading. "In fact, I should start out by saying I'm sorry about everything that happened between us. I've done a lot of things wrong in my life, Susanna."

Like leaving me? she wanted to scream.

Mary seemed to read her thoughts because her hand came up and squeezed Susanna's arm.

"I thought perhaps we could speak, Susanna. You and me. That I'd come over to your *mamm* and *daett's* place this morning. See if we could take a walk down to the pond like we used to. Talk in private for a few minutes, and then I'd stay around for the Thanksgiving meal later in the week. I know I'd have to eat separately, but that doesn't bother me any longer. I've changed a lot, Susanna…since I've seen you last. Worked through some of my bitterness, and I have a lot of things I want to tell you. But now that you're here, I don't have to visit your parents' place. We can talk here."

He can still talk, that is for sure, Susanna thought. Matthew always could run rings around Herman in that department. But her situation had changed now, and the sooner she told him, the better. She tried to look him in the eyes, but her gaze shifted to the floor. Her voice came out way too weak, but at least the words did come. "I'm a married woman now, Matthew. There's nothing we need to talk about. And Mary and I have work to do."

"Oh!"

Susanna felt his gaze burning into her face.

"I didn't know," Matthew finished.

"Well now you do," Mary said. "And I mean no disrespect, but I think you should go."

Matthew smiled. "Do I get lunch before I'm thrown out again?"

Mary's fingers tightened on Susanna's arm, but she said nothing. Apparently she was leaving it up to her to say something.

"No one threw you out, Matthew. You left on your own." Susanna tried to keep her voice from shaking, but a tremor escaped.

Matthew must have heard and his eyes lit up. "I'm sorry. Of course, that's right. It was all my fault. That is what I'm trying to work through. Taking responsibility for my actions. And perhaps making some things right that I've done wrong."

"So you're thinking of coming back to the community?" Susanna asked. What a mess that would be—Matthew living right among them.

He tilted his head. "I'm trying to find healing. That's important, you know. Not burying things in the past. I thought spending time with my family over Thanksgiving…and speaking with you would help me along that road."

"We really have to get busy," Susanna said. "And I'm sure Mary will fix you lunch when it's time. Then perhaps you can be on your way again."

"There's Ernest coming now!" Mary let go of Susanna's arm and raced for the door. She didn't stop, flinging the door open and running out into the yard to meet the buggy.

"You really should go," Susanna repeated as they watched Mary's retreating figure. "It's not going to work, Matthew. It's over between us."

"So you really are a married woman?"

"*Yah.*"

"That's hard to imagine."

"It's not imagination, Matthew. It is what is."

"For how long?"

"A few weeks."

"Oh, so that's why you still look so…so unmarried."

"I'm married, Matthew. And I love Herman. You might as well accept that."

"Herman? Herman Wagler? I'm surprised at you, Susanna. I always thought you liked boys a little more dashing. What happened to that?"

"I'm not talking about this with you." Susanna turned and retreated to the kitchen. A kettle of water was boiling furiously on the stove as steam poured into the air. With a leap she jerked it off and set it in the sink. Now why did she have to run out on him like that? Matthew will only take it as a sign of weakness. He still knew her well enough to know that. And it didn't make things easier. He was seeing way too much already—and probably imagining the rest. It was hard telling what Matthew was thinking or what he planned to do.

She was not giving in to any of his schemes, whatever they were. She had withstood the temptation to follow him into the *Englisha* world, and she would also make it through this. The hardest thing would be telling Herman about Matthew's visit. It was clear he now had to be told. There was no keeping this a secret. Not if Matthew stayed for lunch, and she helped prepare the food. Not even if she left right now. Word would get around, and Herman would be hurt worse by hearing about Matthew from someone else. How could the man do this to her? Matthew was thinking only of himself, as usual. In Matthew's world the sun had always risen and set on himself. He had no idea how much harm he was doing to all of them. And all for nothing.

Susanna paused to listen for sounds of footsteps behind her. Surely Matthew wouldn't follow her into the kitchen. Not when she was in here alone. Not after what she had just told him. Even he had to have that much decency. She was a married woman now.

Four

Under the hiss of the gas lantern that evening, Susanna placed the water glasses on the table. The winter sun had set moments before, the glow of the sunset still on the horizon. In the stillness, she would be able to hear Herman entering the washroom. She would have time to make sure there was a smile on her face before he opened the door.

Should she even tell Herman about Matthew? She'd felt sure at Mary's place about the matter, but the question had been racing through her mind all the way home and even while she rushed to fix supper. Matthew had made them all late getting started with the Thanksgiving preparations, though he had left after the lunch Mary prepared. Then they were able to work quickly to catch up.

At least Matthew hadn't tried to eat at the table with them. He had taken a seat without complaint in the living room with Mose and Laura. Ernest had taken his plate into the living room too, sitting in the recliner, which had helped keep the children's questions at bay. Questions such as why their uncle wasn't eating at the kitchen table with the rest of the family.

Susanna had even been a little thankful for the *bann*. Eating with Matthew sitting near her would have brought back too many memories of family gatherings where they had been seated side by side. Seated around tables and laughing with her parents, siblings, aunts, uncles, and cousins. A situation she had expected to be repeated a thousand times after she married Matthew. Which had turned out not to be.

Family gatherings…Her thoughts went back to this morning. Now some of those meals would never happen at all, given Herman's feelings about Christmas. He would come to Thanksgiving and be happy with the rest of them, but on Christmas Day they would be home as if it were any other day.

So…did Herman really need to be told about Matthew? Would Herman think something was still going on between Matthew and her, even though there really wasn't? Surely not. Herman wasn't exactly the romantic type, so he wouldn't be inclined to think anything was awry. She was, after all, married to him. And for that reason, *yah,* she needed to tell him. Wives shouldn't keep such things from their husbands. Even harmless things that didn't matter. This would be a chance to practice closeness with him.

Placing the last of the food on the table, Susanna paused to catch her breath. Everything looked perfect—just the way she wanted it. Now if Herman would just come in. She'd seen him heading to the barn not fifteen minutes ago. He should be done putting the horses up by now. Perhaps if she went out to meet him, he would hurry.

With a quick glance at the steaming food, Susanna rushed out the door. The air had chilled during the time she'd been home. She wrapped her arms around herself. She should have grabbed a coat, but, really, this will only take a moment. Running toward the barn, she pulled open the barn door. Herman was reaching for the lantern on the ceiling hook.

"Supper's ready!" she sang out, smiling at him. "The food's going to get cold if we wait."

"I'm coming," he said, returning her smile. He looked tired from his day's work.

She drew close to him. Reaching out, she gently took the lantern from him and set it on the floor. Then taking his hands in hers, she noted they felt rough and cold. She rubbed them between hers.

Herman's smile widened. "I thought you might still be sore at me."

"Not really. Not enough to feed you a cold supper."

His whiskers where he'd shaved had grown since this morning, and they would tickle tonight when he kissed her. But she liked that. His little stubble of a beard would soon reach down much further. The few weeks growth since the wedding hadn't amounted to much yet.

When he didn't say anything, she pulled him toward her, tilting her face up, looking into his eyes.

He gave in, wrapping his arms around her and pulling her in close to him.

He did love her, there is no question about that, she thought as their kiss lingered.

"My!" he said, letting go. "I don't think I need any supper after that."

She laughed. "You're not fooling me. A man has to have his supper. Unless you don't like my food all of a sudden."

"Next to your kisses, your cooking is the best thing in this world."

"Oh you flatterer," she teased. He didn't always say things like that. So perhaps he was still trying to make up for this morning.

"It doesn't mean I've changed my mind since this morning." He took her hand in his. "I still stand firm about Christmas."

"I know you do. I guess every couple has to fight about something," she said, pulling him toward the barn door.

"As long as you keep kissing me, I'll settle for that," he said, reaching down to grab the lantern and swinging it with his free hand.

"There will always be plenty of those."

"You sure you're not trying to butter me up? Tempt me into changing my mind?"

"We're still honeymooners, Herman. Isn't that reason enough for kisses?"

He answered with another quick kiss.

"Come." She tried to pull him into a run toward the house. He laughed, playing along before dropping her hand and racing past her. She slipped on the cold ground but caught herself in time. He was already halfway to the house. Throwing herself forward into a fast sprint, she hurried. Herman was inside the washroom by the time she arrived. "That wasn't fair!" she teased.

He laughed as he washed in the basin. She watched while he dried his face and hands. *Nee,* he isn't quite as handsome as Matthew, but almost. A flush spread over her face at the thought. I'm not comparing Herman to Matthew, Susanna corrected herself silently. Not really. The thought came all by itself. It meant nothing. Thankfully, the lantern light wasn't giving Herman a *gut* look at her face, especially if she stayed in the shadows. And if Herman did notice, hopefully he thought she was flushed from the quick run into the house.

Pushing past him, she went into the kitchen and took a quick look around. The food was probably a little cold by now, but they would make do. She had taken up more time by running out to the barn than she would have by waiting for Herman here, but it had been a *gut* idea—greeting Herman like that. Some things were more important than hot food.

"Sit!" she told him when he came through the doorway.

"Bossy, are we?"

"In the kitchen a woman is always in charge," she said, joining him at the table.

"To that I can agree."

He closed his eyes, a smile still on his face, and began praying the short prayer he usually gave at mealtimes. She listened, liking the sound of his voice. It wouldn't grow old, she decided. Even after hearing it every day for whatever time *Da Hah* allowed them to live together as husband and wife.

"So how was your day?" he asked when he raised his head.

"Okay." She tried to sound chirpy. Matthew would have picked up on the tension in her voice, but Herman didn't seem to notice.

He helped himself to the food, piling his plate high. She followed his example, although the portions were smaller on her plate.

"Not hungry?" he asked.

"Oh, *yah,* I'm hungry."

"You must have worked hard with Mary on the Thanksgiving menu all afternoon."

"We did. We were delayed some, so we had to rush."

He was looking at her while he ate, and she knew now was the time to tell him about Matthew.

"You're not expecting, are you?" he asked.

She jumped. "Not that I know of," she said hurriedly.

He shrugged. "That can throw a woman off her food, I hear."

"I do have something to tell you though," she whispered.

A smile crept across his face. "So you suspect it then. Even if you don't know for sure."

"No, Herman. It's something else. Matthew was visiting at Mary's place today. He came in late last night. Mary didn't have time to let me know, or I wouldn't have gone over there."

"Matthew?" Herman's face was blank for a moment.

She looked away as his comprehension dawned. "Matthew Yoder is here? In the community? And you spoke with him?"

"I couldn't help it, Herman. He was right there. I had to."

After a long moment, he shrugged. "I guess there was no harm in it. He left you a long time ago."

Silence settled over them.

After what seemed to her like forever, Susanna said, "I have forgotten him, Herman." She softly touched his arm and looked at the stubble on his cheek.

He didn't meet her gaze. "I know, Susanna. I trust you."

"Herman, Matthew was a long time ago, just like you said. There's nothing between us now. He just wanted to speak with me. He didn't even know I was married."

"And you told him?" He still wasn't looking at her.

"Of course, Herman."

"Is he gone?"

"*Yah,* he left right after lunch."

"So he stayed at Mary's for a meal. Isn't he in the *bann?*"

Susanna nodded. "He ate in the living room while we ate in the kitchen. The children, they were with him. And Ernest went into the living room with his plate."

Herman didn't comment.

"Ernest is Matthew's brother, Herman. They couldn't just turn him out."

He nodded. "*Yah,* I guess so."

"You're not jealous, are you, Herman?" She reached out for him again. "Because you don't have to be."

He smiled, touching her fingers. "I think any man would be jealous of you, Susanna. It's just the way it is with us men."

"But you don't have to be." She begged with her eyes for him to believe her.

He stood and kissed her on the forehead. "I figure I'm married to you and Matthew isn't. Something for which I am most grateful." He smiled.

"There…" She tried to kiss his cheek, but he had moved on. "I will always love you, Herman. You don't have to worry about that."

"I'm jealous, not worried," he said over his shoulder before disappearing into the living room.

At least he wasn't upset. But she hadn't done anything for which he should be upset. She loved Herman the best she could, and soon she would love him a whole lot more. Already her wish was coming true. She would just have to give him more kisses once she was done with the dishes. That would make up for the shock of Matthew's appearance. Herman would like that.

Five

Herman had his head stuck deep in a farming magazine, but the words weren't taking shape in front of his eyes. He was listening to the sound of Susanna cleaning up after dinner. The soft click of the dishes hitting each other blended with the splashing of water.

He ought to help Susanna, he thought, instead of sitting in here trying to read his magazine. But his *daett* had never done such a thing that he could remember, and he could hardly imagine Grandpa Wagler helping Grandma in the kitchen.

It wasn't what men did. At least his *mamm* had always implied they didn't. They worked hard in the fields all day. They came in at night to a well-prepared supper and rested so they would be fresh for another hard day's work tomorrow. Women's work was for women. That was what he had been taught. But now there were other feelings stirring in him. He wanted to help—more to be with Susanna than anything else. Surely drying the dishes for her wouldn't be out of order. Maybe his *daett* had done the same thing when he had first married…before the babies started arriving.

He would try, he decided. If Susanna made a face at him, he could pretend he wanted a drink of water and beat a hasty retreat. She might be brooding in the kitchen even now over their argument about Christmas this morning.

The way she had been acting all evening wasn't what he had expected. Even with her waving to him from the buggy. Susanna had been genuinely upset this morning. That was understandable in a way, but after all, he had warned her that Christmas was something his family didn't celebrate. And they weren't alone either. There were a few older families who agreed with his family. Some of these families traced their lineage clear back to the 1846 founding of the Amish community in Kalona, Iowa.

Back then, December the twenty-fifth was the *Englisha* time for celebrating the Christ child's arrival. The Amish believed Old Christmas in January was the true date. But over the years, some of the families had changed their minds. Influenced by *Englisha* emotionalism, *Mamm* claimed. And the Wagler family was having nothing of it. January sixth was the real date, and the Waglers were holding their ground.

Of course, *Mamm* had never fully explained to him what holding the line would entail. Like telling Susanna they wouldn't be attending her parents' Christmas breakfast. Who would have thought so much emotion was involved? Last year Susanna could still go, even if he wasn't with her. This year they were married, and it wouldn't look right for Susanna to attend by herself.

Herman started to stand and head for the kitchen, but he paused to listen. All was silent now. Susanna must have finished. He had missed his chance tonight. Well, perhaps it was for the best. She might think he was changing his mind about the Christmas breakfast if he chose tonight to offer to help in the kitchen for the first time.

Herman settled back in his chair. Susanna would be out soon. Sitting on the couch near him, her presence comfortable and soothing. Already they made an excellent couple, he thought. Just like he always knew they would. He had even had such thoughts during the years she was dating Matthew. He had often caught his eyes going in her direction at the Sunday night hymn singings— even when he figured she was promised to another man.

Always he had kept himself in check, trying to drive thoughts of Susanna away. He had even thought to ask other girls home a few times, but he never got beyond the thinking stage. People said he was slow in making up his mind or, in unguarded moments, referred to the stubborn Wagler streak that all the family members were reported to have—an accusation not without justification.

Now he was sure it was *Da Hah* who had given him grace to keep waiting until the time was right. When Matthew left for the *Englisha* world, getting himself placed in the *bann*, Herman began to woo Susanna at once.

It hadn't been easy though—the winning of Susanna's heart. Susanna had said no the first three times he'd asked her home, but she agreed on the fourth try. Perhaps to shut him up, if nothing else. But then maybe not, because she allowed him back the next Sunday night…and the one after that.

He had taken his time, never pushing too hard. And Susanna had come around. The moment to ask her to become his *frau* became clear to him the night she first leaned against his shoulder in the buggy. But even then he had waited a few more weeks.

And when she said *yah*, he had even dared kiss her. His first kiss ever, although he was sure it wasn't for her. Susanna seemed to know much more about kissing than he did. That was fine. He wasn't a jealous man. He was a simple man who satisfied himself with the end result. And Susanna was now his *frau*. That was something Matthew couldn't say, even if he had kissed Susanna first.

Herman looked toward the kitchen and listened again. It was still silent. Susanna should have been out by now. Should he go and see where she was? *Nee*, he decided, his thoughts drifting away again. It was best if he gave her time to think through things. This had, after all, been a difficult day for both of them. She would come in when she was ready.

The morning's *kafuffle* had troubled him more than he wished. Not that he would change any of his actions. A man had to stand firm on his convictions or his family would end up who knew where. And surely there was going to be a family soon. Susanna would make a *wunderbah* mother, and he hoped to be a great *daett* for their children.

They would love each other. He had grown up in a loving family. *Daett* leading the way in a life that was pleasing to *Da Hah*, and *Mamm* supporting him. True, *Mamm* could be a little bossy sometimes. But all of them stood together against the many temptations the world had to offer. He wanted that kind of home. And from how Susanna was acting, she did also. Her brief anger had been just a momentary weakness that she was trying to overcome. He could tell, and he was thankful *Da Hah* had given him a *frau* he could truly love and cherish. That was a great gift indeed.

Maybe that was why Matthew's visit troubled him more than he wanted to admit. He didn't think it would bother him at first, but now he wondered. Did Susanna still have feelings for Matthew? In a way it would be understandable if she did. They had, after all, been together for a long time. Had he been hasty in rushing Susanna into marriage? He didn't think he had pushed that hard. Yet what did he know about a woman's heart? Maybe there was more to it than he knew.

And how did Matthew have enough nerve to show up like this—and to speak with Susanna? It sounded like the two had been quite free as they spoke with each other. Not that Susanna really said so, but he could tell by the sound of her voice. They had spoken at length. And about things that would have made him blush had he been there.

She had told Matthew she was married now. Did Susanna sound disappointed when she'd told him? Regretting perhaps that the handsome Matthew couldn't be her husband? Wishing things had turned out differently? It would have been only natural if she had—and also understandable. But that didn't mean Susanna had done those things. He must not accuse her regarding a falsehood without proof. Surely Susanna saw the value of life among the community. And she had chosen that life long before he'd made his desire to take her home known. He had made sure of that.

Nee, Herman thought. Even if Matthew had shown up only to try his hand at luring Susanna into the world, it would never work. He was sure enough of Susanna not to worry about that. And surely Matthew didn't have plans to rejoin the community. Or did he? Susanna would have mentioned that. He would have picked it up in her eyes if she expected to see Matthew again. But there had been none of that.

He really needed to trust Susanna. And he did trust her. But the kitchen was still silent. Laying the magazine aside, he quietly walked to the door opening. Susanna was leaning over the sink, all signs of the dishes gone, but she was still holding the drying cloth in her hands. She seemed fixed on something outside the window.

Walking in his stocking feet he slipped in beside her, pulling her close. He saw her face break into a smile out of the corner of his eye. But there were also tears on her cheeks.

"Is something wrong?" he asked. "I was waiting for you."

"Just watching the stars. They're really bright tonight."

He leaned closer to the glass. "*Yah*, they are. Do you know much about the stars?"

She shook her head. "I just look at them sometimes. It seems like heaven comes closer in those moments."

"I'm sorry about Christmas, Susanna. I know it must be bothering you. Is that why you're crying?"

Her response was to lean against his shoulder.

"I have to do what I think is right."

"I know," she choked out. "But it's so hard, Herman. I'll be the only one from the family who's not there when *Daett* reads the story of the Christ child's birth. And when we sing 'Silent Night.' It's not even in English, Herman. That song was first written in German. Celebrating Christmas is not drifting into the world like your parents think."

"We can't go," he said, not relaxing his hand. And she didn't stiffen at his words. "I'm sorry, but I can't. I have to lead our family in the way I was taught."

She leaned into him and sobbed on his shoulder. He ran his fingers through her hair, pushing back her *kapp*.

"I'm trying hard to see things your way, Herman," she whispered. "So don't hold my tears against me."

"I don't," he said. "I understand."

"You do?" She looked up at him.

"Maybe not completely. But I'm trying."

She nestled against him again. "I've made my own Christmas wish, Herman. Do you want to hear it?"

He hesitated but soon whispered, "*Yah.*"

"That I will completely see things your way by the time Christmas gets here. I think *Da Hah* will help me. Even if I shed a few tears along the way. Because you're the best husband I could ever have."

"You shouldn't say that," he said, touching her cheeks. Not adding the question that flew through his mind. Even Matthew? Susanna had a golden heart, and he should not defile her mind with accusations that were not true.

"I will say them as often as I wish," she said. "Come, I'll make popcorn tonight. It's not that late, and you can enjoy your magazine better while eating popcorn."

"I was reading just fine," he protested.

Susanna smiled. "Really? I think you were sitting there thinking…just like I was in here."

He dropped his head. "*Yah,* I was." She could read his thoughts much too easily.

"Then we will be happy now and thankful for each other. I have been blessed with a very *gut* husband."

"You are too *wunderbah* for me," he said.

She shook her head and then said, "Go now. I'll be there in a little bit with heaping bowls of popcorn."

Six

The late-morning sun peeked through the fast-moving clouds as Herman and Susanna drove toward her sister Mary's place. Bishop Jacob was walking from the barn to his house, and he waved as they went past, his face wearing a broad smile.

He would be happy knowing Herman and she were working through their problems, Susanna thought as she returned his wave. Not that she would ever tell him about them, but if he did somehow find out, Bishop Jacob would doubtlessly approve.

She glanced up at Herman's face as he drove down the slope of a hill. His beard was growing longer by the day, as if it had been waiting for years to escape the razor. He was looking more handsome all the time, she decided.

"A little chilly this morning," Herman said, giving Susanna more of the buggy blanket.

"*Yah*," she said, nestling up against him, all warm and cozy under the warm covering.

"Looks like snow," Herman commented as he noted the clouds ahead of them.

Susanna snuggled closer. "It's cold but a little early to keep snowing. It's only Thanksgiving."

Herman stuck his head out the buggy door, laughing as a few flakes came floating out of the sky to whirl past his hat.

"Those were snowflakes indeed!" Herman pulled his head back in. "Early or not."

"Christmas will be here soon," Susanna added without thinking.

He didn't say anything, and Susanna stayed snuggled up against him. She didn't wish to start this argument again this morning. Not on Thanksgiving Day…and not ever, really. She was going to learn from her husband's good sense in keeping to the old ways. That was all there was to it.

And there was so much to be thankful for on this day, and for all the days of the year. Herman was already providing well for her. He had worked steadily on his fall plowing yesterday, even as Bishop Jacob and his son-in-law completed theirs. In a few days Herman would be done. Quite an accomplishment for a young married farmer just starting out on his own. That Herman would be finishing so soon after experienced people such as Bishop Jacob and his son-in-law was impressive.

"I have a lot to be thankful for," Susanna said out loud, just in case Herman was still thinking about her Christmas comment.

"We both have a lot to be thankful for." Herman smiled down at her.

Apparently he wasn't upset with her. She hadn't said a word about Christmas since that evening by the sink earlier in the week.

Ahead of them Mary's place came into view. Susanna sat up straight, and the buggy blanket on her side slid to the floor.

"I can't believe this!" she whispered.

"Believe what?"

There, alongside the barn, was Matthew's car. It was unbelievable! He wasn't even making an attempt at hiding it behind the barn today. How was she going to explain this to Herman? The whole day was ruined or worse. How did Matthew dare do something like this?

Herman was looking around, his face puzzled, his grip tight on the reins.

"That's Matthew's car beside the barn," Susanna explained.

Herman didn't say anything at first. He looked the bright blue car over as they approached.

"Did you know about this?" he finally asked.

"*Nee.* I thought Matthew was gone for good."

"Well, I guess we'll just have to deal with him." Herman turned into the driveway.

"Like how?" Susanna glanced up at her husband's face, wild thoughts racing through her mind. Did Herman plan to cause a scene and chase Matthew off? He had admitted being jealous, and she could understand that. But making a scene wasn't something her family did.

A slight smile played on his face. "I'm not going to do anything rash, so don't worry."

Susan sighed in relief. "You don't have to worry about me either. Matthew means nothing to me."

"*Yah,* I know." He brought the buggy to a stop by the barn. The blue car sat not ten feet away, a few snowflakes on the hood from the brief blast earlier.

Susanna climbed down and helped unhitch, stealing another quick glance at the car. Did Herman really know how fully her heart was his? Surely he did. But he still looked worried. Should she wait for him here while he took the horse into the barn? She usually didn't, and he would notice if she did now. But going in she would risk meeting Matthew without Herman along—an encounter she didn't wish to make. She would wait for Herman, she decided. He would understand.

Herman led Bruce into the barn. Susanna knew he would put some hay into the stall for his horse. She waited patiently, and when the barn door swung open and Herman came out, she saw the surprised look that formed on his face at the sight of her. "I thought I'd wait for you," Susanna said, trying to smile.

He nodded and led the way to the house.

Oh, what a royal mess this is! Susanna groaned silently. And to have this happen on Thanksgiving morning—the only holiday of the season she was allowed to spend with her family. This was just awful. And now Herman thought she was afraid to face Matthew on her own. At least he looked like that's what he thought, judging from how grim his face was.

Taking his hand she squeezed it. Thankfully he squeezed back, but he still looked grim. Well, this would just have to be a grim day. Matthew had no right to put them both through this.

Mary met them at the washroom door, a pained look on her face. "*Gut* morning." She pasted on a quick smile. "It's so nice to see the both of you."

"Why is he here?" Susanna hissed.

Mary's eyes flew back and forth between their faces.

"*Yah*, he knows," Susanna whispered. "I told Herman everything the other day."

"Oh," Mary managed. "Then that's *gut*."

"But it's not *gut* that Matthew's still here," Susanna insisted.

"He's Ernest's younger brother. I can't turn him out if Ernest wants him staying." Mary's face begged for understanding.

"It's okay," Herman said. "We understand. Don't feel badly about it."

Relief flooded Mary's face as both Mose and Laura came flying out the door and into Susanna's arms.

"Uncle Matthew is here today again, just like he was the other day," Laura gushed. "We'll get to eat with him all by ourselves on the couch again. *Mamm* said so. Isn't that *wunderbah*?"

"*Yah*, I'm glad for you," Susanna said, untangling Laura's arms from around her neck. "When's Matthew leaving?"

Now why did she ask the little girl that question? Susanna wondered. Already words were slipping out of her which shouldn't, as they seemed to whenever Matthew was around. How in the world was this day going to end?

"I don't know," Laura was saying. "I hope he never leaves! He's so much fun to have around."

"Come, now." Mary pulled on her daughter's arm. "Both of you go play with your cousins so Susanna and Herman can get settled in. They'll be here all day."

Laura and Mose raced off as Mary said, "Here, I'll take your coats." Herman handed his over after Susanna slipped hers on Mary's arm.

Please stay with us, Susanna begged with her eyes, *so we don't have to meet Matthew by ourselves.* But Mary had already scurried into the kitchen, leaving them alone. Inside there would be a group of people sitting around on the couches waiting for them. And Matthew would be in the midst of them.

"Come." Herman squeezed her hand again. He led the way through the kitchen opening, and they entered the living room to hollered greetings.

"The young lovely couple themselves."

"They still look alive."

"I can't believe it. They haven't eaten each other yet."

"That's what love can do, you know."

"Now…now…give 'em a little break. They'll grow up eventually."

Susanna figured her neck was growing red from the teasing, and she lowered her head. Meeting Matthew could really mess things up, she worried. She shook hands around the circle, following Herman. *Where is Matthew?* she wondered. *He has to be here somewhere. And we're almost around the living room.*

When Ernest stood up to shake their hands, smiling from ear to ear, Matthew's face became visible from where he'd been sitting behind his brother's chair, keeping his head down.

Now he stood and offered his hand to Herman. For a moment it looked like Herman wasn't going to take it. Then he nodded and extended his hand. "*Gut* to see you again."

"*Yah,* and you too."

"Staying around long?"

Matthew shrugged. "Depends when Ernest kicks me out of the house, I suppose."

Herman didn't say anything, turning to move on. Susanna knew she had better do something soon or everyone would be looking at her—if they weren't already. Matthew could be making things easier by offering to shake her hand, but as usual he wasn't.

"Hi," she said, nodding.

"*Gut* to see you again," Matthew said, looking at her for the first time. He looked tired, his eyes weary.

Susanna rushed past him, following Herman to sit on empty chairs set up along the wall. They were still much too close to Matthew, but there was no other place to sit. Matthew was watching her. She squirmed. Thankfully no one seemed to notice as the chatter in the group continued and lifted to a still higher volume when more of the family arrived. *Mamm* and *Daett* arrived last, going around the circle and shaking hands with everyone. They were as jolly and happy as they could be.

No one seemed uncomfortable with Matthew in their midst, Susanna observed. They had accepted him, as they should. Being nasty to shunned people wasn't the way to act. *Mamm* and *Daett* had always insisted on that. There was little chance of winning people back who had left, they said, if you were mean to them.

But that didn't mean they had a right to stare at you, Susanna defended mentally. Especially if they used to be your boyfriend. She was married now and belonged to Herman. Matthew had no right to look at her for long periods of time. Herman might think she was doing something to attract the man's attention.

"I'm going out to the kitchen," she whispered in Herman's ear.

He nodded, looking relieved.

So he had noticed. Making her way through the crowd of people, Susanna found Mary and *Mamm* working in the kitchen. Several aunts from both sides of the family were also standing around. Clearly there was no work that needed doing. Still, she was not going back into the living room. Not until Herman moved someplace where Matthew couldn't see them.

"So how's married life?" Ernest's sister Betsy asked, a big smile on her face.

"Very *gut*." Susanna smiled back.

"You make such a nice couple," Betsy said.

Susanna held her breath for a moment. This was, after all, Matthew's sister talking. She had always seemed happy about the match with her brother when Susanna had been dating Matthew.

"I told Matthew myself that he was making an awful mistake by letting you get away," Betsy continued, not seeming to notice Susanna's discomfort. "But he has such a thick head and had to do things his own way. Now look at the mess he's in."

Susanna still didn't say anything. What was there to say?

"He's now planning to straighten out some things," Betsy continued. "Even plans to stay around awhile. I hope he does, for all of our sakes. But I'm glad you didn't wait for him. You've found a decent man, if I must say so myself."

"Thank you," Susanna whispered. That was some compliment coming from Betsy. But what did she mean by Matthew planning to stay around for a while? Before she could ask, Betsy moved away and was soon out of speaking range in the crowded kitchen.

Seven

The long, oak dining room table spilled into Mary's living room, extended to its maximum by extra leaves brought down from the attic. Ernest and two of his brothers had set them in place, grunting and teasing each other the whole time. Mary had hovered over them, hollering out instructions.

"Don't break the edge, Ernest!"

"Oh no! You'll scratch the surface."

"It fits in if you don't push too hard."

With all of Mary's attention to the task, the other sisters had held back from overloading their men with instructions. Herman helped move the other furniture back against the living room walls, watching the antics with an amused look on his face.

The look had fled away the few times Herman's eyes glanced over to Matthew, who was still staying in the background.

Now that the tablecloth was down and the whole length ready to fill with delicious products from the kitchen, all of the sisters on both sides had pitched in, making the task an easy one.

"The food's ready," Susanna heard Mary whisper to Ernest.

Ernest fumbled with his hands, apparently nervous now that the time had arrived to speak. There wasn't much he had to say, but for some men even a few words in public brought out the sweat on their upper lips.

Susanna could imagine Herman in the same situation, but he

46

wouldn't be nervous. He just wouldn't. She had never seen him take charge of a large family gathering, but Herman sweating like Ernest didn't fit at all. A cloud passed over Susanna's face. They probably never would have a large family gathering at their place. Not with Herman's feelings about such things. He seemed okay today, but having all this food spread out in their house might be another matter. With *Da Hah's* help she would adjust and not give these things so much meaning. And she was probably allowing the bitterness of the Christmas disappointment to cloud her judgment. Herman, after all, had little against Thanksgiving.

"Ah…" Ernest began. "It's Thanksgiving morning, of course. And…well, we are glad you could come." Ernest's glance strayed over to his brother Matthew for a moment before looking away. "We're thankful for all the *gut* things *Da Hah* has given us this year. All of us have our health, I think. Except for the little things, which we won't go into."

There were a few chuckles around the circle. Susanna had heard the story from Mary herself. How Ernest had been in bed with a bad case of the flu only a few weeks ago—an illness that had lasted more than six days, keeping him out of the fields—a subject he was still embarrassed about. Ernest considered such a lengthy down-time over the winter flu a sign of weakness and an insult to his manhood.

"But we are well now," Ernest continued, seeming to lose some of his nervousness. "And we're living in a blessed land where we have freedom to worship *Da Hah*. This we can always be grateful for, something about which our forefathers could only dream of. So here we are, with our *fraus* and our children gathered around us."

Ernest choked up for a moment, and his nervousness returned.

Susanna saw Mary squeeze his arm and noticed Ernest visibly relax.

"So let's sit at the table. The married folk out here. There are places set up in the kitchen for the children."

There was a rush of children out to the kitchen while the adults found places around the oak table. Mary hurried about, making sure everyone had found a seat.

"You don't have to be shy," Mary told one of the aunts who was contemplating whether to sit beside one of her brothers-in-law. "He's not going to bite. We have the turkey for that."

"I'll protect her if John steals her turkey," her husband said. "I always could handle John in our wrestling matches growing up."

This produced hoots of laughter.

"Oh really?" John shot back. "Do you want to head out to the barn after lunch and see if you can back up those bold words?"

The older brother chuckled but didn't say anything.

"I think John's grown a bit since those days," John's wife, Esther, said.

This brought hollers of encouragement from the men.

"That a girl."

"Stick up for your man."

"Now, now!" Ernest protested from the front of the table. "Everyone settle down so we can have prayer."

A hush came over the room at once and spread into the kitchen. Susanna looked around from her place near the living-room window. Had Matthew gone into the kitchen? He wasn't at the dining room table, which he shouldn't be. But she hadn't seen him leave for the kitchen, though he must have. Now if Matthew would stop disturbing the rest her life, they would be okay.

"Let's all bow our heads in silent prayer," Ernest said.

Silence settled over the house, broken only by a few chair squeaks from the kitchen. The children must be having a hard time holding still, Susanna figured. But they would settle down soon with the *gut* food they'd be eating.

"Amen," Ernest said, breaking the silence. All the people raised their heads. The noise level increased at once in the kitchen and spread back into the living room.

"Start the turkey now," Mary was saying, getting up from her place beside Ernest to see that her orders were followed.

"And the gravy…take plenty. We have more in the kitchen."

"You'd better sit down and eat yourself," one of the sisters told Mary. "Relax, we're all doing fine."

"Oh, these gatherings get me all in a tizzy," Mary admitted, looking like she was going to heed the advice. But at the last second she looked toward the kitchen and dashed out there.

Maybe I should go and help Mary, Susanna thought. There were older girls who could do the job, but Mary might still need someone else. Half rising from her chair, Susanna remembered Matthew. He was out there. Susanna sat down again. She shouldn't be out in the kitchen if there was a chance he was there.

Herman looked sideways at her with a puzzled look on his face. He apparently wasn't used to seeing her bouncing up and down like one of those *Englisha* jack-in-the-boxes. But then she wasn't used to it, either. Matthew was causing all of this confusion.

"I just thought I'd go help Mary," she whispered to him.

He thought about that for a moment in his slow way, no comprehension dawning on his face.

Susanna almost whispered to him, *It's because of Matthew I'm not going.* But Herman was figuring it out on his own, judging by the frown spreading over his face. Now what am I supposed to do? Confound that Matthew!

There was only one answer. She had to face this thing, and Mary really did need help in the kitchen or she would have been back by now.

She smiled at Herman the best she could and whispered, "Mary needs help, I'm sure."

Herman didn't look happy, but at least his frown was gone. He knew she loved him, and if he doubted it, she would show him with extra kisses tonight.

A smile teased the edges of her mouth on the short walk to the kitchen. Matthew might not have intended this, but Herman was getting more of her attention with him around than he would have without Matthew's presence. But Matthew probably wasn't thinking of either Herman or her. He would be thinking of himself, as usual.

Wiping the smile from her face, Susanna plunged into the kitchen. The noise level was twice what it was in the living room. It had also grown quite warm. Mary, along with two older girls, was getting ready to head out to the living room table, their hands filled with food dishes. All of them had flushed faces.

"I'm going to open the window!" Susanna hollered in Mary's ear as she passed.

Mary nodded, looking relieved either from the thought of fresh air or from the arrival of reinforcements. Mary did get into a real tizzy on family days. Maybe it would go better for her as she grew older and did this more often. Not that long ago *Mamm* had handled all of their gatherings, but now the burden was being passed on to the next generation. It could even be this Christmas that one of the daughters would be asked to take on the duties instead of *Mamm* and *Daett*.

Susanna pushed the painful thought away as she jerked open the kitchen window. For a few moments she stood still, allowing the cool breeze to blow over her face. Turning around, she noticed Mary giving her a grateful smile. Then Susanna caught sight of Matthew sitting at the table with the children. He was looking at her with a sorrowful expression, as if his last friend had died and he was all alone in the world.

Susanna looked away at once. Matthew and his condition didn't concern her. If he didn't want to stay in the *bann* and eat in the kitchen with the children, he could visit Bishop Jacob and straighten up the matter. Of course, that would entail coming back to the community. Then perhaps he would find some Amish girl who would take him after his wild life among the *Englisha,* and they could start a new life together.

"How are they doing in there?" Mary asked as the two older girls disappeared into the living room.

"Okay," Susanna answered. "You shouldn't be out here."

"Well, someone has to see after the children and load the food dishes."

That was true, but Mary needn't be out here for very long. Mary needed to eat her meal. Neither did she, thought Susanna as she looked back at Matthew, who was still watching her as he ate.

As if to make a point, Matthew motioned for her to come over. He might need a food dish refilled, Susanna figured, so she walked toward him. This would look less conspicuous than refusing his summons. The children would really wonder if she did that.

"We have to talk," he said, when she was near enough to hear him. "Afterward…sometime…outside."

"No," she quietly answered. "I have nothing to say to you."

"But it's important," he insisted.

Thankful now for the racket, she leaned closer to him.

"I said no, and I mean no. I've said all to you that I'm going to say."

His face fell. "Don't you care if I work through my problems or not?"

She hesitated…and he noticed.

"I'm going to speak with Bishop Jacob this week. It would help if I also could speak with you."

"No," she said, pulling away from him. She was not going to give in. She had nothing to say to him that hadn't already been said.

Mary was staring at her when Susanna stood up. There was no way Mary could have overheard the conversation, but she must have guessed it wasn't about food.

Susanna took ahold of Mary's arm and whispered, "I have to get out of here, and I'm taking you with me. If you don't eat something soon, you're going to pass out."

Mary hesitated.

"*Yah,* you're coming with me. Okay, children!" Susanna raised her voice. "Quiet down."

A blessed silence occurred.

"Everybody has to settle down," Susanna continued. "You can talk a little if you want to, but keep it low. There's way too much racket. And I want the older girls to refill the bowls when it's necessary. But I don't think you'll have to—it looks like there's plenty of food here already. Then we have pies for afterward—pumpkin and cream. You can have one piece each and no more. So no shoving! And Matthew here will see that everyone behaves. Okay?"

There were a few groans. Probably over the one-piece quota of pie, but mostly there were smiles. Even children liked order, Susanna observed. Matthew had a big smile on his face when she glanced at him. He probably thought she was weakening in her resolve to speak with him because she put him in charge. But she wasn't. He had just seemed like a handy tool to help keep order.

"Come!" Susanna pulled on Mary's arm. "Let's go eat."

Eight

As Betsy carried leftover food back into the kitchen, Susanna grabbed a broom and started sweeping the living room. The task would be repeated later, she figured, but why not go over at least a portion of the floor now? It would keep her busy. There were already plenty of women helping in the kitchen.

The men were outside, gathered in the yard in little clumps. Through the window Susanna caught movement inside the big, open, double barn doors and paused to look closer. Why would hay be floating around inside the barn? As she watched, little pieces were flying through the air, followed by a muffled shout.

And she realized she wasn't the only one looking. The men in the yard were all gazing in that direction now. And while they were all staring, Ernest appeared in the barn door, hollering something. Broad grins spread over the men's faces, and they moved en masse toward the barn.

"What did he say?" Mary asked, coming to stand by Susanna.

"A wrestling match, I think," Susanna said. "Looks like John is testing his theory on whether he can best his older brother or not."

"Men!" Mary muttered. "They're all boys at heart."

"Do you want to go out and watch?" Susanna asked. She wouldn't go, but maybe Mary wanted to.

"Of course not!" Mary sounded horrified.

Susanna laughed. "I'm glad Herman doesn't feel a need for such antics. He's more mature than that."

More women had gathered around the window, and Mary didn't respond to the complimentary comment about Herman or repeat Susanna's remark.

Mary could say the same thing about Ernest, Susanna figured, but it might make some of the other women feel bad about having their husbands still considered boys. All men had their faults in one way or the other. Herman had his, with his hang-up over Christmas celebrations. Women just had to learn to live with the faults of their men…as did husbands with their *fraus.*

Outside in front of the barn, the group of men parted. John and his older brother came rolling out of the door. First one and then the other was on top. Susanna heard a gasp behind her as John's brother got a firm grip on John's shoulders and pinned him to the ground.

"Come on! You can get out of it!" John's wife, Esther, declared, as the group of women watched in silence.

Moments passed and John's strenuous efforts to throw his brother off went nowhere. Even with his wife's encouraging words called from the house. Finally he flopped his arms against the ground and gave up.

The group of men stepped back as John's brother let him go. The two stood and slapped each other on the back a few times. The men broke up into smaller groups again. The women around Susanna did the same, moving away from the window. Susanna stayed rooted to the spot, staring. Just inside the barn door, obviously not paying much attention to the wrestling match, were the forms of Herman and Matthew. They appeared deep in conversation. What did those two have in common? Herman didn't make conversation easily. She couldn't imagine what he would say to a man who was in the *bann,* not to mention a man she had once loved. Is that what they were talking about? Could it be? Herman wouldn't bring up such a thing with Matthew. And Matthew wouldn't have anything to say to Herman about their time together, would he? That just wasn't done. And she hadn't done anything wrong during those years anyway. She had nothing to be ashamed of if Matthew was talking about their dating years. Sure she had been sweet on him, but that was no secret. Why else would she date a man for that long?

"Is anything wrong?" Mary asked, having come back to stand beside her.

Susanna jumped and gasped. She shouldn't have made this so plain for Mary to see. Now she too would wonder why Herman and Matthew were talking.

"Did John or his brother get hurt?" Mary asked, peering in the direction Susanna had been staring.

Susanna forced herself to look. Relief flooded through her. The two forms were gone.

"I think they're both okay," Susanna offered.

"So what were you looking at?"

"It doesn't matter," Susanna said. "It's been such a wonderful day, hasn't it?"

"*Yah…*" Mary was still looking toward the barn. Finally Mary turned away from the window. "Well, speaking about a *wunderbah* day, how about you and Herman having the family's Christmas breakfast this year?"

Susanna swallowed hard. Why hadn't she told Mary about Herman's problem with Christmas while she was alone with her the other day? Because of Matthew, that's why. All the *kafuffle* of seeing Matthew had driven the thought from her mind.

Mary smiled, patting Susanna on the arm. "I'm half teasing, Susanna. You don't have to turn so white. I just thought it would be perfect to have our newlywed couple host the day. Sort of add all the sweetness of your new love to the mix. Of course, not that we older married folks don't love each other, but being newly married is such a special time in one's life."

Susanna glanced behind her. Thankfully the other women had

gone into the kitchen and were busy cleaning up the last of the dishes. Now would be a *gut* time to break the news. Mary was an easy one to talk to, and waiting would only make everything harder.

"I think Christmas breakfast had better be at *Mamm's* as usual. Because…I…I don't think we will come this year," Susanna managed.

Mary looked at her as if she didn't believe what she'd just heard.

"*Yah,* you heard me right," Susanna added. "Herman has a problem with Christmas celebrations. He thinks it's following the *Englisha* ways. He believes the time should be celebrated on Old Christmas only—and then very quietly. His whole family believes that way."

"Oh," Mary said, comprehension dawning. "I suppose when I think about it, I do remember that. The Waglers are one of the few families in the community who feel that way. And last year Herman didn't come. I'd forgotten."

"Herman hasn't forgotten."

"Susanna," Mary had her by the arm now, "you don't mean… really…like you and Herman won't come?"

"I'm afraid so." Susanna looked away.

"But there must be some way. Will Herman let you at least come?"

"He's my husband, Mary. I'm not coming without him."

Mary groaned. "This will be quite a shock to the others. You know how much the day means to *Mamm* and *Daett*. Won't Herman consider that?"

"It's our new tradition against their old one. And you know which will win out, don't you?"

"So you've talked of this at length…" Mary let the sentence hang.

"*Yah,* and I'm ashamed of the fight I put up," Susanna said. "I've made it my Christmas wish to learn my husband's new ways and make them truly my own."

"You're a saint, Susanna, but this is awful. Christmas morning will never be the same without you. What are we going to do?"

"Carry on as usual. You know an Amish man's mind is hard to change."

Mary groaned again but said nothing more.

"Speaking of an Amish man," Susanna said. "There's Herman coming with his horse. We must be leaving early."

"He doesn't look happy," Mary said, staring across the lawn at him. "Do you think he doesn't approve of the men wrestling? Could that have upset him?"

"I don't think so," Susanna said.

Mary ignored Susanna's denial. "Oh no! If Herman's upset, maybe you won't be able to attend Thanksgiving gatherings again. Tell him Ernest and I are very sorry this happened at our place. It won't ever happen again."

Susanna shook her head. "He's not that way, Mary. He's a decent man. He's not going to forbid me from coming to the family gatherings on Thanksgiving Day because of a wrestling match. His parents celebrate Thanksgiving. Not quite as elaborately as we do, but they get together."

Mary looked relieved as she followed Susanna to the bedroom to help her find her wrap.

"Aren't you going to say goodbye to everyone?" Mary asked when Susanna draped her shawl over her shoulders and headed for the front door.

"We're going a little early. They'll think something's wrong if I…"

"*Yah,* I understand," Mary said, opening the front door for her. "It's better this way. I'll say your goodbyes for you."

Without looking back, Susanna hurried across the lawn. The men were still standing around the barn door, a few of them helping Herman hitch Bruce to the buggy. She climbed into the buggy and sat down. Moments later Herman threw her the lines, hollered goodbye to the men, and got in. They were off.

Susanna tried not to move as they pulled out on the main

highway, and the steady beat of Bruce's hooves on the pavement settled around her. Was Herman upset or not? She didn't dare glance at his face to check, and he obviously wasn't going to say anything.

"It was a *gut* day," she finally ventured. It seemed a safe enough thing to say.

"*Yah,*" he said, adding nothing more.

His voice sounded okay, so Susanna stole a quick glance. *Nee,* there was something wrong. She could tell by the set of his jaw. Maybe he hadn't liked the wrestling of John and his brother after all.

"Did the men wrestling bother you?" she asked. "Their horsing around?"

"Not really," he said.

Herman sounded like he meant it. Then what is bothering him? His talk with Matthew? That must be it. Should she admit she'd seen them together?

As they rode in silence, Susanna's mind raced with questions. If she said nothing, would Herman ever mention what the talk with Matthew had been about? Would that be *gut*? Did she even wish to know?

As Bishop Jacob's place came into view, Herman solved the problem. "Matthew had some things to say to me today."

"Oh?" Susanna tried to keep the tremble out of her voice.

"Sounds like you and he had some *gut* times together."

"But Herman..." She turned toward him. "You know I dated him for a long time. Of course we were sweet on each other and enjoyed some good times. Why would Matthew tell you this though?"

Herman shrugged, not looking at her.

"Herman, please. I love you. You know that, don't you? Matthew has no right to come into our lives like this. Why was he talking with you anyway?" she asked again.

"He says he's trying to find peace. Matthew sort of rambled on and on about the past. I don't know. I guess he thought I should hear about it."

"But Herman, this isn't right. I have forgotten about those times."

"He said he has a ring of flowers you made for him one summer down by the pond. Keeps it pressed in a book to this day. Matthew hopes *Da Hah* will let him love again like you and he loved each other."

"Oh, Herman, this is so wrong!" Susanna grabbed his arm. "Why would Matthew be telling you this?" she repeated.

"So you do remember the flowers?"

"You must not believe everything Matthew says, Herman. Please."

"So there was no ring of flowers?"

There was no use holding back the information, she decided. The quicker she said something, the better. "*Yah,* Herman, there was. But it means nothing now. I made them for a special occasion so many years ago. And Matthew kept them—I can't help that."

"Kept them perhaps as a memory of the special occasion?"

"I'm sure, Herman, but it has nothing to do with today...with us."

"I know," he said, pulling into their driveway.

Nine

Herman pushed open the barn door, pausing for a moment to glance back at Susanna's retreating form. She was almost at the house, walking with her head bowed. Was he being too hard on her? But how? He had every reason for discomfort and for questioning. She had once loved the man. And why was Matthew spilling such intimate secrets into his ear? Yet he had to be honest. Matthew's words had seemed more like musings than anything else. Perhaps they really were just the memories of a troubled man seeking peace with his past.

That Susanna had dated Matthew for several years, he knew. That they had been sweet on each other—quite sweet, that they had planned to marry, Herman had known, so why did it bother him to hear it from Matthew?

Herman led Bruce inside the barn, pulled his harness off, and turned him loose in the field. Toward the west he noticed dark clouds hanging low in the sky. Snow clouds, no doubt. Early this year. They might even get another light dusting tonight, from the way things looked.

Watching Bruce take a lumbering run around the pasture, shaking his mane Herman wondered, was his young marriage in trouble? How could that be? Susanna loved him, didn't she? It certainly appeared so. Even with the trouble over their different family Christmas practices, she was being a model of submission and virtue, although she did have that initial flash of anger. It was understandable Susanna should struggle with letting go of what she was used to. That was normal, and they would surely adjust.

But Matthew's words were troubling. But it wasn't just Matthew. It was the side of Susanna Matthew had shown him. Matthew probably hadn't intended that, mumbling on and on about the good times he and Susanna had once had.

"I'm not saying things could have turned out differently between us," Matthew had said. "Because they couldn't have. I could never give Susanna what she deserved. A home among the people. A place she felt safe in. A husband who didn't always have ideas about leaving…" Matthew's voice had trailed off.

Herman had tried to be patient, not understanding why he was being told this. He was willing to listen if it soothed Matthew's obviously troubled spirits.

"Very early on, I think I knew Susanna was too *gut* for me, but I couldn't bring myself to pull away from her. She was so alive and so in love with me. And if I let myself go, I imagined the same thing for me. But in the end, our relationship was all imagination on my part. It could never go much beyond our evening drives home in the buggy with her snuggled under the blanket next to me."

Herman had winced at that line. Susanna hadn't done much snuggling up to him when he drove her home during their dating years. But she did now. He had always taken her reserve before their marriage as virtue, but apparently it hadn't been. Had her feelings for him changed after the wedding? Or was she reliving a love from the past when she nestled next to him? Perhaps she was trying to recapture what she'd lost?

He looked at the dark clouds in the west and shook his head. He was a simple man with simple tastes. These things were too deep for him. The heart of a woman was a mystery he'd never given much thought to, but now it seemed to matter a whole lot. Something hurt inside his chest that had never throbbed like this before.

As he looked around, the voice of Matthew came drifting back. "The moment I finally knew it was over was at the most unexpected time. I never told Susanna this. In fact, it took me months to get enough courage to admit to myself that it was over for us. That we could never be what she wanted us to be."

Herman had said nothing as he fiddled with a piece of straw. He apparently wasn't expected to say anything. The words were spilling out of Matthew.

"It was on a summer Sunday afternoon. We had taken a walk down to the pond behind her *daett's* place. Susanna had never looked so lovely as she did that day. I could hardly look at her, awestruck by thinking she might really become my wife. The moment has finally come, I thought. This is what I want to do more than anything else in the world. Marry this woman. Have her by my side for the rest of my days. So what if I have doubts about giving her what she wants? Love would be more than enough. I gave myself to the emotion of the moment—which I now know is all it was."

Herman had waited. Clearly there was more to come, but he hadn't been sure he wanted to hear this. What Matthew was already saying was hurting things inside of him he hadn't even known were there. But he had remained silent and Matthew continued.

"I asked her to marry me that day, Herman. Down by the pond. And she said yes. She was so happy it hurt. That's what finally woke me up. Her happiness. The joy on her face. The me she saw. But the Matthew she loved wasn't who I really was. That day I understood, but I was unable to admit the truth. She went into the side of the woods and picked flowers—little tiny ones, purple, orange, and blue. Wove them into a circle for me. 'A circle of love,' she said. 'Our love.' And she gave them to me." Matthew's voice trailed off again, a faraway look in his eyes. "I'm sorry," Matthew had said moments later, looking up for the first time. "I guess I shouldn't be telling you this. But I just had to get it off my chest. Perhaps find my way again. I can't share this with anyone else."

"You could come back to the church," Herman had managed to get out. "That would be the first step toward peace." A simple answer, he figured. Not like the complicated stuff Matthew was telling him, but Herman didn't have any other ones. He was a simple man.

A brief smile flashed across Matthew's face. "I might go down and speak with Bishop Jacob. Confess some things to him. Not that he's going to lift the *bann* on me, but for my own sake before *Da Hah*."

"You can always come back," Herman repeated. There hadn't seemed anything else to say.

Matthew shook his head. "I thought I might try that when I came back this week—well, before I arrived actually. But then I found out Susanna had married. Deep down I always knew coming back wouldn't work, so I'll take Susanna's marriage as an added sign from *Da Hah* that He knows me better than I know myself. The way to the past is closed, Herman. I finally told Susanna that months after that afternoon by the pond. And now I know it's still true."

Herman had nodded, not because he necessarily agreed, but perhaps it was best this way. Having Matthew around would be mighty uncomfortable. But Matthew's absence was a horrible thing to desire because his soul was in such danger. Herman's thoughts came back to the present. Right now he couldn't help how he felt about the matter. And there was nothing more to think or to say about Matthew.

He really needed to get inside before Susanna thought something was amiss. On the way out of the barn, he paused and looked at the stack of hay piled against the wall. Perhaps he should throw more bales down from the haymow? The job needed doing soon, and it would give him time to gather his thoughts before facing Susanna again.

Yah, I will, Herman decided. He climbed the ladder. Dusty silence greeted him on top except for a few chirping sparrows on the beam high above him. Spider webs hung everywhere, but that wasn't unusual. He must stop thinking dreary thoughts. Susanna waited for him inside, and she was his *frau.* No matter how much Matthew wished it otherwise.

That was the real problem, wasn't it? Matthew wished he were married to Susanna. *Yah,* Matthew might not wish to admit to the fact, but deep down he did. Matthew wished things had turned out differently. That he had stayed in the community and taken a different road in life. Surely that was his real reason for being here now—to find out if there was a way back to the Amish life.

Did Susanna also feel this way? Herman sat down on the hay bales, the thought heavy on his mind. Was this true? It couldn't be. Susanna wasn't like that. But she had changed since their wedding, hadn't she? Into a person not unlike the one Matthew described. Warm, loving, kind-hearted, snuggling up to him whenever she had a chance.

Was she trying to make their relationship like hers and Matthew's would have been? Or used to be? A warm memory in her mind that wouldn't go away?

Herman stood and threw a bale of hay down the ladder chute, listening to it bounce on the floor. With a great heave, he threw another one and then another one. This time the strings burst and hay flew everywhere, blocking the chute.

"Stupid," he muttered to himself. "You've never acted like this before."

But then he had never been married to a *wunderbah* woman like Susanna, who apparently had a lot of secrets in her life. He was growing into a jealous man, which wasn't what he wanted at all.

Yet the hurt around his heart was growing worse. And the more he thought about Matthew and Susanna, the greater the pain.

And she had made the ring of flowers for Matthew after he asked her to wed him. Of course, that was perfectly natural for Susanna. She had no way of knowing Matthew wasn't who he said he was. But she had never made one for him, even after he asked her to wed. She hadn't done anything like that.

Pushing the hay out of the ladder chute with his hands, Herman dug his way through. Coughing from the dust and knocking his hat off, he jumped part of the way down. Slapping off the worst of the hay, he picked up his hat and walked toward the barn door. Once outside he took quick steps across the lawn. Susanna had the gas lantern burning in the living room even though it wasn't quite dark yet. She meant it as a welcome sign, and a smile crept across his face. He had to stop this worrying. Susanna would make popcorn tonight. Maybe he could talk her into adding caramel as a special treat. For what, he wasn't quite sure—maybe for surviving encountering Matthew today and still loving each other.

Thankfully he hadn't spoken harsh words to her on the way home. He had tried to speak gently even though his heart was throbbing with the memory of Matthew's words. And he would never tell her what he knew. It wasn't necessary. He would trust Susanna. Her love for him was as real as his was for her.

With a broad smile on his face he opened the front door, the light flooding his face. Stepping inside he looked around, seeing no one. Where was Susanna, he wondered. Hearing a muffled sound from the kitchen, he hurried in that direction.

Susanna was sitting at the kitchen table, staring out of the window, and sobbing with great choking sounds.

She wasn't waiting for him. *Nee,* she too was full of memories. No doubt memories of Matthew. Seeing him today had brought them rushing back. Surely that was the cause of her tears now. As he retreated a step, Susanna must have heard and turned to face him, her handkerchief clutched in her hand.

"I'm sorry," he mumbled.

She said nothing, the tears still running.

Herman turned and beat a hasty retreat back to the barn.

Ten

Susanna sobbed as the sound of the front door closing hung in the house for long moments. At least Herman hadn't slammed the door. Wasn't that what men did when they were really angry? Herman hadn't looked angry at all. More heartbroken than anything, she decided. And that was why she should be running after him right now. She should have jumped to her feet when he came to the kitchen doorway, but her feet had been stuck to the floor.

The turmoil was too much. Matthew's return. Matthew wanting to speak to her. Matthew talking to Herman. And likely now Herman knowing more than she had ever planned on telling him.

Matthew had told him about the ring of flowers. And if that had been said, a lot more had probably been said. She had only to think about the long time Herman had stayed out in the barn to know that...and how disturbed Herman had looked on the ride home.

Why didn't she respond to Herman a moment ago? For the first time since their wedding, she hadn't rushed into his arms. Had she done something wrong today? *Nee.* Not even back in the days when she was so in love with Matthew. She had done nothing wrong. Her feelings had been real, and in some ways still were. Was that the problem?

Yah, it was. But what was she supposed to do about that? If only Matthew hadn't come along right now she would have been okay. She had been doing so well since the wedding. Learning to know and appreciate who Herman was. And slowly the feelings of love had been growing. She was sure of it. But now this. Did Herman know too much to ever trust her again? That was the awful question. Wiping her eyes, Susanna thought of Matthew and the days when they had been together. Everything had looked so easy back then. The world colored with feelings of love and light. How innocent she had been, believing everything Matthew told her. Accepting everything about him as real. But she had based her love on something that wasn't solid. And Herman was so different. So very solid. Herman had character, and he was patient, and kind, and very real. There wasn't a thing about Herman that was fake. He probably couldn't pretend if he tried. Which meant that Herman had to be deeply hurt to have turned and walked back to the barn like he just did. And it also meant he wouldn't easily be won back. There was no use running after Herman right now with him knowing what he did. Wrapping her arms around his neck and kissing him would only remind him of the tales Matthew had told him.

Why did Matthew have to come right now? Why not next year, or the year after that? When her love for Herman had grown deep and solid. When it could stand this kind of storm. Not four weeks after their wedding when they barely knew each other.

What if Herman stayed out in the barn all night? It was cold out there, and he didn't have a blanket. Would she dare take one out for him? Or would he reject even that? What about tomorrow? Where would he eat if she didn't feed him? Would he go somewhere else for the day? Tell others about her relationship with Matthew?

Surely not! She must not imagine things like this. She must make supper for Herman. The best she could prepare in the shortest time. And Herman would see the light in the kitchen. He would know what she was doing and return. His hunger would drive him, if nothing else. And if that failed, she would go to him. Beg him to forgive whatever she had done to hurt him. He loved her kisses. She knew he did. She would love him again, and he would respond like he always had before.

Rushing about the kitchen, she lit the extra lantern and hung it on the nail in the kitchen ceiling. Racing to the living room window she glanced out toward the barn. Everything was dark, but Herman was in there somewhere. Probably sitting on a hay bale or pacing around thinking of her. He had to be there. Surely he would be coming in soon.

Running back to the kitchen Susanna began her work, heating the leftovers she had. That would have to do, she figured. Preparing food from scratch would take too long. And they already were full from the Thanksgiving dinner. It wasn't food they needed right now, but love.

While the food was warming in the oven, Susanna made popcorn. Heaping the bowl full of fluffy white kernels, she placed it near the oven for warmth.

Now what else could she do? She paused to look around. Didn't Herman like candied popcorn? *Yah,* he did.

Grabbing the caramel, she heated it over the stove and then ran long streams of the sugary mix over the popcorn. With the lid slapped on, she shook the bowl for a long time. When she opened it, the golden mixture brought a smile to her face. Herman would love this. This popcorn would chase away whatever dark thoughts were crowding in.

Opening the oven door she checked the food. It wasn't quite done yet, she decided. A few more minutes were needed. She would see if the living room was in decent shape while she waited. It had been clean this morning, but perhaps something had fallen out of place.

A quick look around revealed nothing amiss, but Susanna still grabbed the broom to give the floor a fast sweep. When she was done, she went back to the oven. She took the warmed casserole dish out and set it on the kitchen table. Slicing the bread, she placed a few pieces beside Herman's plate, along with his favorite jam—blackberry. His mom's recipe and quite delicious. As *gut* as any they'd ever made at home, she had to admit.

Taking the basement stairs two at a time, Susanna brought up a jug of apple cider. One of the few she had brought from home after the wedding. This was a special occasion. She would replenish their supply the next time she was at the market in Kalona.

Surely Herman would be in soon. Taking slow steps back to the living-room window, she peered out. The barn was still dark, but Herman had to be out there somewhere. Did she dare go after him? She had to. She couldn't wait and let the food get cold.

He was probably waiting for her anyway, brokenhearted, thinking she was still in love with Matthew. And that wasn't true at all. She was in love with him, with Herman. Even in the middle of this wild *kafuffle*. Matthew had never been real. She was seeing that more clearly all the time.

Opening the front door, Susanna ran across the lawn. The barn was dark when she pushed open the door and stepped inside. Peering into the darkness, she could see nothing. She needed a flashlight. Herman might be in the hayloft, and there was no sense in her making things worse by breaking her legs getting up to him.

Perhaps if she would call, he would answer. "Herman!" she yelled, her voice squeaking. "Herman!" She tried again, louder this time. But there was still no answer. She felt her way around the barn with her hands.

"Herman! It's Susanna. I'm sorry...I wasn't trying to ignore you in the house."

Bruce banged in his stall, recognizing her voice, but the rest of the place held only silence.

I can't go on without hurting myself, Susanna decided. She felt her way back to the barn door and raced toward the house; almost tripping on the porch steps but catching herself in time. A skinned knee was all she needed now. Blood running down her leg at a time like this.

Finding the flashlight in the washroom, she ran back to the barn and searched. Herman wasn't on the main floor of the barn, so he must be in the hayloft. Taking her time she climbed up, sending the flashlight beam all around the stacked hay bales. No Herman. Perhaps he is sitting behind the stacks, his heart too broken to speak?

Climbing all the way up she searched. No Herman. She went down and out to the silo. No Herman. He was gone, no question about it. Cold stabs of fear ran up and down her back. Her fingers felt frozen as she clutched the flashlight. Out in the yard she shined the light around the barnyard. What had she missed? Was there someplace else Herman could be?

There wasn't. And here she was acting like he was some lost child she had to find. He wasn't a child. Herman was a man, her husband, and he was gone. Should she run up to Bishop Jacob's place? If she did, they would all look at her with pity. Only married for a few weeks, they would think, and already quarreling with each other.

They wouldn't come to help find Herman because Herman wasn't lost. He had left because he wanted to leave. She had to face that, no matter how much it hurt. She went back into the house. The casserole had cooled. The popcorn stared back at her from the place by the stove, accusing her: "You chased your husband off…"

"I did not," she whispered. "I did not! I love him, and he loves me."

Then why is Herman out there somewhere, and you are in the house alone? The food didn't have to ask the question this time. She asked it herself.

Walking into the living room she sat down and buried her face in her hands. There had to be something she could do. Search the woods perhaps. Call his name again and again. When she found him she'd tell Herman she loved him. That they could work through this. That she didn't have a desire for things to have worked out with Matthew. That her time and marriage with Herman was so much better.

But Herman wasn't listening right now. Would he listen in the future…once he came back in from wherever he was? He *was* coming back, wasn't he? He wouldn't leave her, would he? Matthew had—and she had never expected that to happen. Was she wrong again?

"Oh, please, *Da Hah!*" she cried out. "Don't let this be happening to me again. I can't take it. If Herman doesn't love me, what will I do?" She heard a noise outside, and jumped to her feet, quickly moving to jerk open the front door. Nobody was in the yard or around the corner of the house. She heard only the wind blowing and saw soft snowflakes floating past.

The snow that had been threatening all afternoon, now it began to fall in earnest. She had been too worked up to notice. Herman was out in a snowstorm! He would freeze if he was in the woods alone. She had to go look for him…but she couldn't. It was a task too great for her, and her heart would break searching in vain among the trees of the forest. Better if she stayed here and waited. Herman was coming back. He *was!* Because he loved her and she loved him.

Shutting the front door, she walked back into the kitchen. Placing the food in the oven, she shut the door and turned off the heat. There was no point in keeping it on. Herman was coming back, but it might not be for a while. He was a simple man, but he was also stubborn. She would pray—that's what she would do.

Taking one last look at the popcorn sitting on the stove top, she went into the living room and knelt beside Herman's recliner.

Eleven

Susanna woke with a start. She leaped to her feet from where she'd been sleeping on the couch. The afghan went flying across the floor. Her head pounded as she paused. She clearly heard footsteps outside the front door. Was Herman returning from wherever he'd been? Holding her breath, Susanna took a step forward as the latch rattled and the door was pushed open.

Herman appeared in the shadowy darkness, his hat and shoulders snow covered. He stopped with his hand on the knob as his eyes searched the room.

With a cry she rushed forward. He opened his arms to her long before she got to him.

"Oh Herman!" Susanna gasped. "Where have you been? I looked all over for you. And you're covered with snow!"

"*Yah.* It's snowing outside."

"You've come home again!" Her voice ended in a sob.

"I had to think," he offered. "I was walking in the woods."

Susanna slid his coat off his shoulders and rubbed his cold hands between hers. "Come…sit on the couch. What time is it?"

"I don't know."

"It's got to be after midnight." Susanna wrapped her arms around him again.

"I'm sorry I left for a while…" his voice trailed off.

"You don't have to say anything." Susanna pulled on his arm. He didn't resist as he sat on the couch with her. She found the afghan lying on the floor and wrapped it around his shoulders, watching as Herman shivered.

"You didn't have to leave," she whispered. "Now you're going to catch a cold."

He shivered again as she nestled against him.

"Are you hungry? I had supper ready, but it's cold by now."

She felt him shake his head.

"But you have to be hungry. I'll warm up something for you."

He didn't protest, so she slipped away to light the kerosene lamp in the kitchen. Maybe as badly as he was shivering, she ought to fix him something hot to drink first and go from there.

Putting water on to boil, she turned the burner up. While it heated, she brought out the cocoa and marshmallows, setting two cups on the counter. She would drink with him, and they could talk after Herman warmed up. He must have been thinking awful thoughts to have wandered around in the woods all this time. Glancing up at the clock, she groaned. It was already past two o'clock. Herman had been out for hours. But he had come home! That was the important thing.

"Come on, come on!" she whispered to the kettle. "Hurry up!"

A watched pot never boils, she reminded herself. She might as well check on Herman while she waited. Taking the lamp with her, Susanna went back into the living room. Herman was still seated where she had left him, shivering violently now. His face was pale in the flickering light of the kerosene lamp. "Herman, you're cold." She sat down beside him. "Why did you stay out so long with only that thin Sunday coat on?"

He didn't say anything and he didn't look at her.

"Oh Herman. I'm so sorry. I didn't mean anything by how I acted when you came in from the barn."

"I'm sorry too," he mumbled.

"Sorry for what? I'm the one who should be sorry."

"I couldn't stop walking," he said. "I was thinking about us. About how you must wish you weren't with me."

"But, Herman, that's not true! I love you."

He said nothing as he shivered under the afghan.

"Herman, believe me. *Please!* I don't want anyone else, to be with anyone else." She ran her hand over his face as the teakettle whistled in the kitchen. Susanna rushed away, returning moments later with a cup of steaming hot chocolate. She would run back for hers in a moment. All that mattered was that Herman warm up.

Slipping the cup into his hands, she searched his face. If Herman would only smile a little, she would know that all was well. But he didn't have the slightest sparkle in his eyes. His face was even paler than it had been when he first walked in. What had she done to him? And all because she'd been crying when he came in from the barn. She'd just needed the release…a little time to recover herself.

Oh Matthew! If he'd only stayed away this wouldn't have happened! But she shouldn't blame Matthew. He was only doing what he thought was right. Her own heart was what betrayed her, and she was so ashamed of that. Herman was a wonderful man, and she wanted to love him with all of her heart.

"Darling," she whispered, touching his face again. He still hadn't sipped any of the hot chocolate steaming in the cup in his hand. She knew Herman loved his hot chocolate. It hadn't taken more than a few days of their short marriage to discover that.

"Is that what you used to call him?" Herman whispered.

With a sob, she nestled tightly against his shoulder. She gripped his hands holding the cup in hers. The hot chocolate spilled over the sides.

"Oh Herman, it's not like that!" she cried, jumping to her feet and dashing into the other room. She returned with a dishcloth.

Wiping both their hands, she clung to him. "It's not like that at all, Herman. 'Darling' doesn't mean the same thing when I use it for you. It's so much better."

He hung his head, not answering. Taking the cup of hot chocolate in her hands, she lifted it to his lips. They were chapped. She hadn't noticed that before. There must be more of a storm outside than she knew. And her husband had been out in it. With a gentle prodding of her hand, he opened his mouth and swallowed. Herman didn't look well at all. Talk would have to wait. She'd better get Herman to bed. Maybe a *gut* night's sleep was what he needed. More than her chattering and vows of love whispered into his ear. He probably didn't believe a word she said at the moment anyway. Not after all the things Matthew had probably told him.

Herman kept drinking, and she kept insisting, "You'll feel better with something warm in your stomach and a *gut* night's sleep. I love you, Herman. Lots and lots! And nothing Matthew told you is like it is now. He's not seeing things right at all. You are many, many times more the man he was or is, Herman. You're more than Matthew could ever hope to be."

Herman still wasn't saying anything. He only stared at the wall, drinking the cocoa when she put it to his mouth. At least he was drinking. That was something to be thankful for. How awful would it have been if he'd been so mad that he'd never come back? Herman had plenty of reasons for being upset. Matthew had no doubt seen to that.

But here she was blaming Matthew again. All the while, Matthew had probably said nothing but the truth. She *had* called Matthew "darling," and "sweetheart," and "my dearest," and other endearments many, many times. And she had kissed him often and with pleasure. All of which Herman had no doubt figured out.

But that was then and this is now, Susanna protested silently. Different in ways that couldn't be explained. Right now wasn't the time to continue trying to convince Herman of her love. He was looking worse by the moment. His shivering hadn't stopped, and now his entire face looked red and chapped.

Running her hand over his cheek, she pulled him close. "Come, you should get into bed."

He didn't protest as she helped him move by pulling on his arm. She set the empty cocoa cup on the desk. Taking his hand in one of hers and the lamp in the other, she led him to the bedroom. He sat on the edge of the bed while she helped him take his shoes off. In the soft light she pulled off his socks. She gasped when she saw his feet were red and icy cold.

"Oh Herman! You shouldn't have stayed out so long!" Her voice caught with a sob. "I love you. I do! I love you so much."

She looked up and saw he was trying to smile, the effort obviously great. "I'm so sorry, Herman," she whispered. "I'll be back in just a minute. Don't move."

Dashing into the kitchen, she filled a bowl with warm water from the kitchen faucet, adding a dash of Epsom Salt from under the cupboard. With another sob, she grabbed a towel out of a drawer and raced back into the bedroom. Herman was still sitting just as she'd left him. Bending over, she slipped both his feet into the water. She lifted one foot out at a time and rubbed, staying at it until the coolness in his skin was gone.

She wiped his feet dry with the towel and then tenderly massaged his feet. When she finished and looked up, a hint of a smile was on Herman's face.

"Thank you," he whispered. "That feels much better."

She almost laughed out loud. Instead she jumped up and gave him a long hug. She stopped in the middle of it, noticing Herman was still shivering. She felt his shoulders shaking.

"Come," she said. "I'll help you under the covers."

He didn't protest when she took his hands and pulled him up.

Once on his feet, he made a halfhearted effort to undress as the shivering increased. She helped him then. With unfamiliar motions, she unbuttoned his shirt and pulled it over his shoulders. Opening the buttons on his trousers, she helped him sit on the edge of the bed while she pulled them off.

A shiver ran through her. Herman would never allow her to help to this degree if something wasn't really wrong. His strong body looked the same, but there was something different. A weakness that had never been there before hung over him.

She pulled back the covers, and Herman slowly slid between the sheets. Susanna covered him with the quilt. Tucking in the sides close to him, she ran her hands over his face. He was still shaking. He needed more blankets. Opening the cedar chest on the other side of the room, Susanna took out the thickest quilt they had and draped it over the bed.

"Can I get you something else?" she asked. "Food? More hot chocolate?"

His face looked flushed now, and she placed her hand on his forehead. It was hot—much hotter than before.

"I'll take some more hot chocolate," he whispered.

"I'll be right back!" Herman looked white as she raced out of the bedroom. What kind of a mess had they gotten into? What if Herman was really sick? Like pneumonia or some other horrible disease? Caught while his defenses were down after he had wandered around in the cold night tormented by thoughts of Matthew and her.

Herman wasn't going to lose her, she thought as she poured water into a cup. And Herman cared about her. That much was plain to see. Herman wouldn't have roamed around in a snowstorm if he didn't care a lot about her. She didn't deserve this devotion, but what a wonderful thing it was. Matthew had never been distraught in the least over whether she loved him or not. He had, in fact, walked away from her love quite willingly.

"Oh Herman!" she whispered again as she took the cup to the bedroom and handed it to him. He was still shaking, even under the quilts. She helped him sit up to drink the cocoa. He drank in quick gulps now and smiled when he was done. "Thank you. I don't deserve this special treatment."

"Of course you do! Don't say that."

His smile faded as he shivered again. Now was not the time for talking. Herman had to be kept warm. Tucking him under the quilts again, she changed into her nightgown and slid under the covers on her side of the bed. Wrapping herself around him, she held Herman until his shivering stopped and he fell asleep.

Twelve

Susanna tossed and turned, her dreams as wild as the winds that blew fiercely outside the windows of the house and lashed the windowpanes with snow. She and Herman were shuddering under the assault. She ought to be cold, even freezing with how much the storm was howling outside the house, but she wasn't. She was burning up. Had Herman left the furnace on high or was the house on fire? With a gasp she awoke, her hand clutching the edge of the bed. "It was just a dream," she whispered, not moving as she looked around the bedroom. Through the window she could see the dawn breaking in a clear sky. The house wasn't on fire, and there was no storm outside. But she was burning hot—the heat was coming from Herman's body.

She sat up, pushed back the quilt, and ran her hand over Herman's forehead. It threw off heat in waves, and his brow was wet with sweat.

She leaped out of bed and dressed quickly. Racing into the kitchen, she ran water from the tap until it reached lukewarm. She filled a small bowl. Grabbing a fresh washcloth, she made her way back to the bedroom. Herman woke while she was bathing his forehead. His eyes were bloodshot.

He muttered, "What's wrong?"

"You're sick. You're burning with fever. You have to stay in bed."

He struggled to sit up but soon gave up.

Susanna held his hand as Herman lay back on the pillow. "If you rest, you'll get better faster."

He nodded but didn't look happy.

"You have to eat something," Susanna told him. "Then maybe you should go to the doctor. You got very chilled last night from being out in the woods."

Comprehension dawned on his face, followed by shadows of a frown.

"Herman, please," she begged. "You don't have to worry about anything."

He struggled to sit up again.

She put her hand on his shoulder. "No, Herman. Let me get you something. You're sick."

He managed to sit on the edge of the bed, but he made no further effort to stand. His face was still flushed and sweaty.

"What can I get you? Chicken soup or oatmeal?"

He shook his head as he lay down again.

"You don't want anything?"

He turned toward her and tried to smile. "I'm okay. But the chores…can you do them?"

"Of course." In the weeks since their wedding, she hadn't done any outside chores. But she'd been in the barn many times, and she'd done outside chores when she lived at home.

"It's just the horses, really. And the calves behind the barn," he added.

"Do the horses get grain in the morning?"

"Not when I'm not working them. Just hay. The grain for the calves is in the bin inside the back door."

She already knew that and nodded. "You give them three buckets."

He looked pleased and smiled for the first time since yesterday.

"I'll go out right away. Will you be okay?"

"*Yah,* but you ought to eat breakfast first. The animals can wait."

"Okay," she agreed. She moved from the bedroom to the kitchen. She had tears in her eyes, and Herman didn't need to see them. They weren't tears from just seeing him lying there so weak and frail, but also because of his kindness. He was thinking of her before the chores.

Wiping her eyes, Susanna fixed a quick oatmeal breakfast. She made enough in case Herman would be well enough to eat by mid-morning. Surely he wouldn't be in bed that long, even with the chill from last night. But then Herman wouldn't be in bed at all if he'd only had a slight chill. He must be really sick. And he hadn't answered her about going to the doctor. She bowed her head in silence and prayed. She ate to the ticking of the clock on the kitchen wall. How quiet things were with Herman sick. It was a strange feeling. She was often in the house alone during the day, but it had never seemed this still before. Having Herman sick was not a *gut* feeling at all.

And it was her fault for not being nice to him when he came in last night. In his mind she must have confirmed his worst fears. None of which were true! Sighing, Susanna went back into the bedroom. Herman looked like he was sleeping, and she almost left without saying anything.

His eyes opened.

"Should I harness Bruce to take you to the doctor in Kalona?" she asked. "I'm worried about you, Herman."

"I'm not that sick," he said. A spasm of pain crossed his face.

"Are you sure?"

"I'll be fine. I just need to rest. And we can't afford it."

"Okay…" She left and closed the door behind her, a tear creeping down her cheek. Herman was right. They didn't have much money. Not after paying the down payment on the farm and struggling with the few bills that had come in. Herman didn't come from a rich family. He was determined though, and she was determined with him. They would make it as farmers.

Still, one had to go to the doctor when necessary. Herman might not admit how sick he was. Not if he was worrying about money. She would have to keep this in mind. Herman was running a fever now, but he could get worse.

After pulling on her coat and boots, Susanna left the house. For the first time she noticed the snow on the ground. There wasn't much, but a decent amount for this early in the year—right after Thanksgiving. Her boots scrunched as she walked and Susanna shivered. This was the snow that had fallen on Herman last night, drifting over his shoulders. It didn't seem that friendly now. Not like snow usually felt. Especially the first decent snow of the year. Normally her spirits would be soaring, and she might even sing a Christmas carol on a morning such as this.

Pain shot through Susanna's heart at the thought. She must not think about Christmas. That was still far away, and this trouble would be over by then. She would live through Christmas morning somehow, even knowing her family was gathered at *Mamm* and *Daett's* house and she wasn't a part of it.

Herman would be well long before Christmas, and they would have things worked out between them. She would make caramel popcorn that day. Surely Herman wouldn't mind eating it with her in the evening after supper, along with cups of steaming hot chocolate. That couldn't be against his family's traditions...could it? They would be together, the two of them, and that would be enough.

As Susanna pushed open the barn door, the horses greeted her with wild whinnies. They were hungry. She rushed to throw them hay from the stack beside the stalls. Herman had several bales ready, so she didn't have to climb into the haymow. And there might even be enough for tomorrow if Herman was sick that long. But surely he wouldn't be.

Behind the barn, the calves stretched as they stood from their bed of straw under the overhang. They didn't look that hungry. She gave them the correct amount of feed and checked on their water tank. The float wasn't frozen, and the water was running okay.

Leaving the calves munching on the feed, she walked back through the barn. From outside, the sound of buggy wheels crunching in the snow reached her. She rushed to the window. Who would be coming at this time of the morning? She gasped at the sight of Deacon Atlee tying his horse at the hitching post. What did *he* want?

She eased open the barn door and stepped outside.

Deacon Atlee didn't seem surprised at the sight of her in work clothes. He smiled and said, "*Gut* morning. About done with the chores?"

"*Yah.*" Susanna didn't offer more. He probably wanted to speak with Herman, but she didn't plan to let him inside the house. Herman didn't need to be disturbed until he was feeling better.

"I see I timed my visit about right. I wanted to get here before Herman started his fieldwork this morning. Is he in the barn?"

"No, he's sick. And unless it's really important, I don't think Herman should have visitors."

"I'm so sorry," he said. "Did this come on suddenly?"

"*Yah,* last night." Deacon Atlee didn't need to know the whole story, she decided. And he wouldn't understand anyway.

"I see," he said. "Well, I will speak with you then. But not alone…"

His voice fell, and he glanced at the ground.

"*Yah.*" Susanna said. This wasn't Saturday afternoon when Deacon Atlee usually came calling on church matters. So they must not have done anything wrong. "Is there something you need that I can help with?"

He didn't answer right away. His head stayed bowed for a minute or two. Finally he looked up. "There's an urgent matter that has come up, Susanna. And I need to speak to you about it. Bishop Jacob is quite concerned and wishes me to clear up the matter with you."

"*Yah?*" Susanna waited. What would bring the deacon out on a Friday morning instead of Saturday afternoon?

"I had hoped to speak with you and Herman together. Do you think we could go into the house and do that?"

Susanna shook her head. "Herman isn't even eating right now. I don't think he should be disturbed.

Deacon Atlee nodded again. "I'm sorry. You did tell me that. Then I will come back later with Lavina. Perhaps this evening would be okay? If Herman is better by then, we can speak together. And if not, we will speak with you alone."

Susanna swallowed hard, her heart racing. Deacon Atlee wasn't known for his shyness around women, so he must have quite a delicate matter to discuss if he wanted his wife along for the conversation. Something of a private nature? Perhaps something Matthew had said to Herman? But how would Deacon Atlee know anything about that?

And Herman hadn't told her anything that might generate a visit from a deacon. Unless he hadn't told her everything. Was there something else that had driven Herman to wander the woods last night?

Deacon Atlee was looking at her, waiting for her response. She nodded as tears threatened to come.

"I will see you tonight after supper then." Deacon Atlee climbed into his buggy.

Susanna stood frozen in place, watching him drive out the lane. Behind him the buggy wheels left long, thin marks in the freshly fallen snow, pocked in the middle by the horse's hooves. It was a beautiful sight, and usually she would have stood there for long moments enjoying it. But right now nothing looked beautiful. Matthew must have said something awful to Bishop Jacob last night about their relationship. Nothing else could explain this sudden visit. With a moan, Susanna walked toward the house. What was she going to tell Herman? And what was she going to do after Deacon Atlee repeated whatever Matthew had said? There was obviously plenty that could be misunderstood. Look at how Herman had reacted already.

Thirteen

Susanna worked in the kitchen all morning, trying to keep the noise down to a soft level even though she had bread and pies to bake. Every thirty minutes or so she peeked into the bedroom to check on Herman. He was still asleep although he was tossing and turning. A few times she slipped in to touch his forehead. He was still running a fever, but it wasn't climbing.

When Susanna eased open the bedroom door around lunchtime, Herman had his eyes open. She went in and sat beside him on the bed. "How are you doing?" She reached down to give him a tight hug.

"Not well," he groaned. "Why does my head hurt?"

"Because you are sick. You got soaked last night wandering around out in the snow. Oh Herman!" She buried her face in his chest.

His hand touched her shoulder and then her cheek. "Don't cry, dear. I'm not blaming you."

"But I am to blame. And Deacon Atlee stopped by this morning. He's coming back this evening with his *frau*."

"With Lavina? Do they know I'm sick?"

"*Yah,* I told him."

"Then they're checking up on us. Isn't that *wunderbah?*"

Susanna groaned. "No, Herman. I don't think so. Deacon Atlee didn't want to discuss whatever he had to say with me alone. It must be something awful. Do you know what it is?"

He shook his head. "Whatever it is, we'll be okay." A thin smile spread over his face.

"May I get you something? You haven't eaten since yesterday noon. You'll be skin and bones before long."

"Perhaps I'll take something," he said.

"Then you *are* getting better." She ran her fingers through his hair. "What about chicken soup? I don't know what else to make for sick people."

"I'll try that."

"With crackers?"

He shook his head. "Just the soup. Maybe the smell will revive me a little."

"Then I'll be right back." She tucked the quilt around Herman before leaving.

Finding the recipe in her cookbook, Susanna heated the water while gathering the spices she needed. Thankfully she had leftover fried chicken from before Thanksgiving that could be used. Herman needed food quickly.

Measuring and stirring the soup together, she heated it to a boil. Pouring some into a bowl, she took the steaming mixture into the bedroom. Setting the bowl and spoon on the dresser, she helped Herman sit up. "Now open your mouth. I'm going to feed you."

He smiled. "I'm not a baby."

"You're sick and I'm taking care of you." Susanna retrieved the soup, ladled a spoonful, and blew on it. "And I want to," she added.

He took the first spoonful eagerly.

"More?"

He nodded.

She continued, and he made no objections until the bowl was empty.

"You ate all of it!" Susanna's eyes were shining.

"I'll be out doing the chores tonight," he said.

"No, you won't, Herman. You don't look well enough yet."

"I suppose not." He lay down again with a sigh. "But I'll be better soon with chicken soup that *gut*."

"So you liked it?"

"*Yah*, of course. You made it."

"Oh, Herman. You shouldn't say things like that. Not after yesterday."

"I was a little out of my head," he said. "But I'm okay now."

She gave him a tight hug, holding on for a long time. He might think everything was going to be okay, but she didn't.

"There's someone driving in right now," he announced.

Susanna raced to the front room window to peer around the drapes.

"It's Deacon Atlee's buggy." She walked back into the bedroom. "He said he wouldn't be back until this evening."

"Bring him in, Susanna." Herman tried to smile. "I'm well enough to see what he wants."

Trembling, she left the bedroom, leaving the door open. It kept her feeling closer to Herman, and she needed all the comfort she could find at the moment. Why did things have to go this way?

Waiting inside until she heard footsteps, Susanna opened the front door. Her eyes widened when only Lavina stood on the porch. Where was the deacon? Susanna glanced toward the parked buggy.

Lavina followed her look. "I came by myself. Atlee said Herman has taken sick."

"*Yah*, he is…or was. I just fed him chicken soup, and he seems some better."

"May I come in?" Lavina asked. "I told Atlee he had no business making plans for this evening with a sick man in the house. He saw my reasoning at once and feels very badly about it. He wants me to pass on his apologies. Sometimes men can be that way, especially when they're on church business."

"I understand," Susanna managed. "Deacon Atlee doesn't have to say he's sorry. Do come in."

Lavina stepped inside, taking off her coat. "Is there anything I can do to help? I know with a sick man in the house you can be so busy the rest of the place doesn't get tended to. And the chores. Do you need help with them?"

Susanna's head was spinning. Lavina was here to offer her help, not to talk about whatever church business was on the deacon's mind.

"Herman's doing okay," Susanna said, much calmer now. "I don't think it's anything serious, but perhaps you could check on him now that you're here." Susanna lowered her voice. "Herman won't go to the doctor, and I've never taken care of a sick husband."

"You'll learn." Lavina smiled. "So where is the sick fellow?"

"In the bedroom," Susanna said, leading the way.

Herman was propped up on the bed when they walked in, apparently ready for conversation with Deacon Atlee and his wife.

"Herman, Lavina came by herself to see if she could help out," Susanna said. "I asked her to check on how you're doing. I don't want you getting pneumonia or dying on me."

"I'm doing okay," Herman stated firmly.

"That's what they *all* say." Lavina ran her hand over Herman's forehead. "Let me see your throat."

Herman hesitated before opening his mouth. Lavina pressed his cheeks together as she peered inside, turning his head toward the light.

Susanna choked back a laugh. Herman being treated like a little boy tickled her immensely.

"Say 'ah,' Herman," Lavina ordered.

"Ah…" Herman responded, as if he was choking for real.

"There now." Lavina slapped him on the back. "You've got some infection down there, but I don't see anything serious. What happened? Did you get wet?"

"I stayed outside a little too long in the snowstorm," Herman admitted.

"Some men don't have a lot of sense," Lavina told him. "But the first snowfall can catch you by surprise sometimes. I always had to keep after our boys during the beginning of winter. But one thing is for sure, a few days in bed with the flu makes most men dress more warmly."

"I think I've learned my lesson for this winter." Herman pasted a smile on his face.

Susanna almost burst out laughing. The effort was so cute, even with Herman still feeling so poorly. He looked like a little boy eating sour candy who was trying not to spit the "treat" out of his mouth.

Lavina wasn't noticing though. "I guess Susanna told you Atlee was here this morning?"

"*Yah,*" Herman said.

"He wants to come back this evening," Lavina continued, "but I'm not allowing it with you laid up sick like this."

"I don't mind," Herman said. "I'll be well enough to hear what he has to say by then. I can't imagine he'd have anything bad to say about us. We've been behaving ourselves." Herman tried another of his sweet smiles.

He's getting better at it, Susanna thought, glancing away. If he caught her laughing, Herman might not be as successful with his charm offensive.

"Well, if you're sure. I'll tell him he can come after supper. And I'm glad to hear you're getting better. When I first heard, I imagined the worst. I could just see a pneumonia case on our hands."

"Thanks for your concern," Herman said with a nod.

"And take care of yourself for the next few days," Lavina lectured. "When one's in a weakened state, that's when pneumonia strikes. Even walking pneumonia isn't something you want to deal with."

"Susanna will take *gut* care of me." Herman flashed his smile again.

Lavina ran her hand over Herman's forehead once more before

leading the way out of the bedroom. At the front door she paused. "I have no idea what Atlee wants this evening, Susanna, as that's not my business. But whatever it is, I can't imagine it's that serious. You two are the sweetest couple around, if I say so myself. I know Bishop Jacob was so happy when he heard you made such a *gut* choice in a husband. After what you went through with Matthew, our hearts all went out to you."

"Thank you," Susanna said quietly.

"You just hang in there, and *Da Hah* will be with you," Lavina said.

Susan opened the door, and Lavina walked out and went toward the buggy.

Watching her climb in and drive off, Susanna took a deep, steadying breath. She closed the door and headed back to the bedroom. Herman was still sitting up, looking serious now.

"Sit down, Susanna," he said. "We need to talk."

"About what?" she asked, her heart pounding. Easing herself down, she sat on the bed.

"Atlee's visit tonight. You'd better tell me about your relationship with Matthew. Everything, Susanna."

She tried to keep breathing evenly. "There's nothing to say, Herman. Nothing you don't already know."

"Maybe, but why don't you tell me anyway."

She stole a quick glance at his face. He looked kind. A little pale perhaps, but that was from his illness. Clasping her hands, Susanna began. "Matthew and I dated for many years, but you know that. I was deeply in love with him, which I hate to admit. I think you already know that too. He asked me to marry him, and I said yes. I never thought we would break up. I kissed him a lot more when we dated than I did when you and I did. That wasn't because I didn't like you. I was just more cautious and the feelings came more slowly. And you didn't seem into that kind of thing very much." She looked at him with a pained expression.

"Go on," he whispered.

"What else is there to say?" she asked. "I loved him, Herman. And Matthew broke my heart. Is that what you want to hear? Do you blame me for that? Do you believe I should have known what kind of man he was? And if you do, then maybe you'd be right on all those points. But I *didn't* know, Herman. I loved Matthew. Is that a sin?"

"Now, now," he mumbled, pulling her into his arms.

She sobbed against his shoulder. "I love *you*, Herman. I want to be the best wife you could ever dream of."

"I know," he whispered into her hair. "But I still have to ask this, Susanna. Were you inappropriate with Matthew at any time?"

She sat up trembling. "Is that what Deacon Atlee wants to talk about? Do you think Matthew said something like that? It's not true, Herman! Believe me."

"I do believe you." He pulled her close again.

Fourteen

Herman was sitting on the couch wrapped up in a quilt. Beside him was a fresh cup of hot chocolate. Susanna pulled on her coat and reached down for her boots. "Will you be okay for a while?"

He gave her a weak smile. "The way I've been mothered all day, I ought to be better by now."

"You deserve it!" she said, sneaking over in her stocking feet to kiss his cheek.

His smiled broadened, and he wrapped himself tighter in the quilt.

"Don't forget the calves need straw for their bedding tonight."

"Straw and no feed." She repeated his earlier instructions as she pulled her boots on. She walked to the door, opened it, and stepped outside. Closing the door behind her, she ran across the lawn. The snow was gone, melted by the noontime temperature, but a chill had returned. The skies looked clear, so it would get cold tonight. Winter was indeed coming early to the Iowa plains. Deacon Atlee would also be coming soon. That was why she was doing the chores a little early. The horses wouldn't mind, Herman had said, and the calves only needed bedding. Herman was being so understanding about everything, and her heart no longer pounded at the thought of the deacon's visit. Whatever concern he had, Herman would stand right beside her. He believed in her. Rushing through the chores, she fed the horses hay. Then she found a bale of straw lying inside the back barn door. Lugging it outside, she shooed the calves away from their bedding area and spread the fresh straw.

"There you are," she told them. "All ready for the cold night. No snow this time, I hope."

Looking toward the tree line across the fields, Susanna shuddered. Herman must have been totally heartbroken to have wandered around in there for hours. And in the snow and cold. It was a wonder he hadn't contracted pneumonia. How the man must love her. It made a person feel warm down to the toes, even with the cool evening wind blowing against her.

A chill ran through her moments later when she heard horse hooves pounding the pavement. Moving through the barn, she closed the door tightly behind her. She ran across the yard. This might not be Deacon Atlee coming, but if it was, she would rather be inside the house with Herman when he arrived.

"I think he's coming," she said in response to Herman's startled look as she rushed in.

He half rose from the couch and then settled down again. "At least take this quilt off me."

"No, you have to stay warm."

"I look like a frog on his lily pad."

Susanna laughed. "Maybe, but I don't care."

"I'm at least putting it across my lap." He pulled the quilt off his shoulders.

"It's him," Susanna said, peeking around the drapes.

"Come and sit down then," Herman ordered, his voice still weak.

She sat beside him.

"You'll have to answer the door," Herman said with a chuckle.

Susanna bounced up again. They were both nervous, Susanna figured, and that would excuse their silly actions. If she passed out in a dead faint once Deacon Atlee came inside, she wasn't to blame for that either. Not in all her growing-up years had the deacon come calling for her. For her brothers, *yah,* but she had always behaved herself.

She waited until there was a knock on the door before opening it with a smile. "*Gut* evening."

"*Gut* evening," he said. "Is it okay to come in?"

"*Yah.* Herman is on the couch in the living room." She motioned with her hand.

"*Gut* evening," Deacon Atlee repeated to Herman when he stepped inside. "I hope I'm not disturbing you."

Nothing but our lives, Susanna almost said, but she sealed her lips. That would be no way to begin the evening.

Herman was motioning toward her while Deacon Atlee was taking off his coat. She was to take the coat, of course. Susanna gathered herself together. She must play the hostess now that she had her own home. That was something new, but it was high time she learned.

"May I take your coat?" Susanna offered.

"Thanks." Deacon Atlee handed it to her.

"Please take the rocker beside Herman," she told him before leaving for the bedroom with his coat. Herman looked pleased as she went by. He must think she was doing okay with her new hosting duties.

"Awfully cold winter we're having," Deacon Atlee said when she came back.

"*Yah,*" Herman agreed.

"Heard you got caught out in it." Deacon Atlee chuckled.

Herman joined in the laughter. "We young people do foolish things sometimes."

"I guess so," Deacon Atlee allowed. "Which brings me to what I came for. I hope this conversation will not overtax you, but it seemed *gut* to Bishop Jacob and me that this matter be addressed at once. I was troubled in my mind when I first heard, but Bishop

Jacob was truly concerned. As you know, he has a high estima-
tion of the two of you. His heart couldn't rest until this matter was
dealt with."

"And what might this matter be?" Herman asked.

Deacon Atlee cleared his throat. "I didn't wish to bring up this
delicate matter with Susanna this morning. Not without either
you or my *frau* present." He paused, as if clearing his mind. "I suppose you know that Matthew Yoder was in the community over
Thanksgiving."

"*Yah,*" Herman said. "He was at Susanna's sister's place—at
Ernest and Mary's house. We celebrated Thanksgiving there."

Deacon Atlee's eyebrows went up a little. "I hope all the proper
rules of the *ordnung* were followed. Matthew is in the *bann*."

Like any of them could forget that, Susanna thought, but she
pressed her lips together and stayed silent.

"We did," Herman answered. "Matthew ate in the kitchen with
the children, but we were respectful to him as Christian people
should be."

"Then you are to be commended," Deacon Atlee said. "These
family situations can get sticky, and rules are easy to overlook
around the holidays. Especially when dealing with someone who
is in the *bann*."

"I'm glad none of my family is in the *bann*," Herman offered.
"And Susanna's family is involved only through marriage."

"I'm glad too," Deacon Atlee agreed, giving Herman a sideways glance.

Herman was *gut* at this, Susanna thought. It was good of him
to remind Deacon Atlee they were both from families who had a
long tradition of upholding the church *ordnung*. This wasn't an
idle point when considering whatever the deacon and bishop had
against her.

"Did Susanna have any contact with Matthew?" Deacon Atlee
asked.

Susanna nodded.

Herman spoke up. "I was there all day at Thanksgiving, and they didn't say more than *gut morning* to each other," Herman said. "Which I think is perfectly in order. They did know each other quite well for a long time."

"*Yah,* I guess you could say so," Deacon Atlee allowed. "But I'm glad to hear that everything was done properly."

"So what is the problem with Matthew?" Herman asked. "Were you and the bishop concerned that Susanna conducted herself inappropriately with him over Thanksgiving?"

"*Nee,*" Deacon Atlee said. "I didn't know about Thanksgiving."

"I see." Herman fell silent.

Susanna almost smiled. Herman knew Deacon Atlee hadn't known about the Thanksgiving gathering, and he probably brought it up to show that he was aware of Matthew and Susan's previous involvement. It had clearly thrown the deacon off his stride.

Herman was now looking quite innocent as he pulled the quilt tighter around himself.

Deacon Atlee noticed the movement and shifted in his rocker. "I don't wish to keep the two of you longer than necessary, but I do need to clear this matter."

"*Yah,*" Herman said, as if he were in perfect agreement. "But I'm still not sure what 'this matter' is."

"Well..." The deacon let out a breath. "Matthew came to speak with Bishop Jacob that evening—on Thanksgiving. Matthew was seeking to clear himself of things in his past. Confessions of a private nature occurred. Feelings of bitterness he had harbored, words they had spoken harshly to each other. Each apologized to the other, and much was accomplished toward better Christian feelings between the two of them."

"Is Matthew coming back to the community?" Herman asked.

"I wish I could report that," Deacon Atlee said, "but I cannot. The progress they made in repairing relationships didn't reach to the level of the church. I doubt Matthew is willing to make the necessary changes to return."

"I agree," Herman nodded soberly.

Susanna would have smiled at Herman's tactics if her heart hadn't been sinking so fast. They were getting close to the real reason Deacon Atlee was here, and she didn't like the direction of this conversation.

"Matthew also shared with Bishop Jacob about the close relationship he used to have with your *frau*, with Susanna," Deacon Atlee said. "Which we can understand, of course, since they were near marriage from what Matthew said. Is that true, Susanna?"

Susanna swallowed the lump in her throat. "*Yah,* we had plans."

"But that was well known." Herman spoke up, obviously protesting the content of the conversation.

He might as well not, Susanna figured. Deacon Atlee was going to carry on and ask his questions.

"We didn't have an inappropriate relationship," she said, not looking at Deacon Atlee. "I'm sorry if Matthew told Bishop Jacob something untrue."

"Matthew didn't say you did anything wrong," Deacon Atlee said. "But the bishop and I wanted to make sure. We hoped with all our hearts there was no basis for that kind of allegation."

Susanna felt her face turning red. Never had she spoken about such an intimate subject except with Matthew and Herman, but she might as well get this over with. "I was once in love with Matthew. This I admit to you, and I have told Herman all about it. But *Da Hah* has changed my heart and kept me from following Matthew into the world. During our time together, we did the things couples do who are in love, I suppose. We held each other, kissed each other, but we were never inappropriate. Neither Matthew nor I wished for such a thing."

"I'm glad to hear this," Deacon Atlee said. "Bishop Jacob feared the worst after his conversation with Matthew. Sometimes things are said that one doesn't know quite how to take. Bishop Jacob was afraid Matthew was holding back a full confession because of his regard for you. I hope you understand and forgive us for feeling the need to check with you."

"It's okay," Susanna whispered, her face still burning. She would be blushing every Sunday for years now, knowing Deacon Atlee had heard her talk about such things. But it was better this way. She had to clear her name, and she also needed to affirm Herman's. He didn't need any accusation hanging over him that his *frau* had been inappropriate before he married her.

"How do you feel about this matter?" Deacon Atlee asked Herman.

"Susanna has been completely open with me on this matter, as well as on others," Herman said. "She has told me about her relationship with Matthew in enough detail to satisfy me, and I have no reason to doubt her."

Susanna could have kissed and hugged him right in front of Deacon Atlee, but that would definitely not help matters.

"Well, Herman, I hope you'll be better soon." Deacon Atlee rose. "And I hope I haven't caused you grief. I know my heart is much lighter, and so will Bishop Jacob's be when I talk to him tonight."

Susanna scurried to the bedroom while Deacon Atlee shook Herman's hand. When she returned, she held his coat for him. "Thank you for coming. I'm glad this matter is over with."

The deacon smiled and pulled the coat over his shoulders. "I wish nothing but the best for both of you. May *Da Hah* give you His highest blessings." He left, closing the door behind him.

Susanna waited until his buggy was halfway out the lane before she climbed into Herman's lap. In relief she sobbed into his shoulder. He wrapped the quilt tightly around both of them.

Fifteen

*E*arly on Monday morning Susanna had her first load of wash on the line, snapping the last piece on with a flourish. She rubbed her hands together, blowing on them for warmth. The snow from last week was gone, but there was still a nip in the air. Clearly winter was setting in early, and Christmas would be here before long.

Herman was recovering slowly. He had insisted on getting up for the chores this morning. She had persuaded him otherwise, convincing him also not to attend church services yesterday. There was no sense in spreading around whatever he had if it was contagious.

"Not everyone wanders around in the woods most of the night in a snowstorm," he'd muttered.

"That just weakened your body's defenses," she'd told him. "You still caught something, and you don't want it passed on." That had been enough to convince him, and Susanna had figured that secretly Herman had been grateful to stay home, though he would have been the last one to admit it. Likely a trait he picked up from his stubborn family. His *mamm* probably took her children to the services even if they were burning up with fever. Susan took a deep breath. She really needed to calm herself. Herman's *mamm*, Iva, was coming over this morning. The way the woman had huffed and puffed yesterday when Herman wasn't in church was enough to chill a body to the bone. Clearly she thought Susanna didn't measure up to her idea of a *gut frau*—either by not forcing Herman to come or by leaving her husband at home sick while she went to church.

Susanna had attended only at Herman's insistence. She could have told Iva that, but she hadn't. What was the use? The information wouldn't have penetrated all the theatrics. Susanna would have desired nothing more than to sit on the couch at home beside Herman all morning, seeing that he stayed warm and keeping his hot chocolate cup filled.

Susanna smiled. Herman was addicted to her hot chocolate. He had sputtered a protest about it last night, sounding a little like his mother. "You're going to spoil me completely. I won't even want to work in the fields after all this mothering."

Susanna picked up the clothes hamper. Her smile lingered. Herman was also becoming addicted to *her,* and that was quite a *gut* feeling. *Da Hah* was answering her prayer. *Yah,* in strange ways, but it was being answered. She was finding a deepening and ever-growing love in her heart for Herman. And the man was so nice to her. He couldn't be any better if he tried. Missing Christmas with her family was a small price to pay for such a *wunderbah* husband.

Halfway back to the basement, Susanna paused. She heard buggy wheels clattering into the driveway. She turned and saw Herman's *mamm*, all wrapped up in a buggy blanket even though it wasn't that cold. Her bonnet strings were tied so tight that her chin bulged. My, the woman was out early. Susanna thanked *Da Hah* that she had at least one load of wash on the line. One less reason for Iva to think poorly of her. But there would be something else, no doubt about that.

Susanna went forward to greet Iva. She was Herman's *mamm* and must be made to feel welcome.

"*Gut* morning!" Susanna sang out.

"*Gut* morning," Iva replied. "How's Herman doing?"

Susanna grabbed the horse's halter as Iva climbed out of the buggy. "Some better. He wanted to chore this morning, but I thought he ought to stay in the house for the day yet. If he overdoes himself, he might have a setback."

"Humph," Iva said. "Herman wasn't raised like that. We only let the children stay in bed if they had over a hundred degree temperature. Even then we didn't make things too comfortable for them. Gives them ideas about ease and pleasure—things *Da Hah* doesn't intend for mankind to enjoy. Otherwise he wouldn't have thrown Adam and Eve out of the garden."

Susanna blinked. Iva had never spouted this freely about her views before. Maybe she'd been saving it for when they were finally alone together.

"I suppose you know how to unhitch a horse," Iva said. "I want to see how Herman's doing."

"*Yah*," Susanna managed, speaking to Iva's retreating back.

The front door opened and Iva disappeared inside, slamming the door shut.

"Well!" Susanna bit her tongue. The woman was a storm cloud—perhaps a hurricane. Patting the horse on the neck, Susanna led him closer to the hitching post before taking him out of the shafts. Apparently Iva planned on staying a while if she wanted her horse unhitched. A long visit meant a long trial. Well, so be it. More time to get to know her and perhaps even come to love her. Already she was learning to deeply love Herman, so maybe she could come to love Iva too. She hadn't thought her Christmas wish might include learning to love Herman's *mamm*.

A shiver ran through her. Iva probably never approved Herman's choice of a *frau*. This would explain the underlying coldness in her smiles. Susanna had always written that off to not knowing Iva that well. And with her heart still hurting over Matthew, it wasn't like she'd had a lot of time to think about Herman's parents and how they felt about her. Herman had been enough to think about.

"Come on!" Susanna jerked on the horse's reins. He protested with a deep groan, and she stroked his neck. "Sorry. I didn't mean to take my anger out on you. It's not your fault you're Iva's horse."

What a horrible thing to say about her mother-in-law! Susanna thought as she dropped the shafts to the ground. She shouldn't be angry at either Iva or her horse. Pushing open the barn door, she led him inside and made sure he had plenty of hay in front of him. He started munching at once, as if he were quite hungry.

"Humph indeed," Susanna muttered, marching toward the house. Iva might think she'd come to take charge, but this was her home. Iva was not going to take over!

Susanna didn't get far before she forced herself to pause and relax. This was no way to approach her mother-in-law. Herman loved his mother and was probably very glad to see her. She would have to act the same way and feel the same way. There was no choice in the matter. Opening the front door, she slipped inside. Loud noises were coming from the kitchen, and Herman sat shivering on the couch, his quilt gone.

"What are you doing!" Susanna exclaimed. "Where's your quilt?"

Herman nodded toward the kitchen, his face pale. "I guess it's time I get up and do some work around the place."

"You will do no such thing," Susanna said, searching for his quilt. She found it thrown on the floor behind the couch. Picking it up, she wrapped it over his shoulders.

A smile played on Herman's face. It vanished when Iva appeared in the kitchen doorway.

"Now there you go!" Iva exclaimed. "That's why he's still sick. If you keep babying the man, he'll never get well. I'm sure Herman hasn't finished his fall plowing yet. I saw the field still half done myself when I drove in."

Herman tried to stand up quickly and groaned.

Susanna pushed him down with her hand. "I'm sure the fall plowing will get done in time. I don't want Herman out there working when he's not well."

"Well, if he doesn't get his plowing done, don't blame me!" Iva disappeared into the kitchen.

Susanna took a deep breath. That had been easy enough. All she had to do was stand up to Iva, and the woman backed down— as she should. Susanna was Herman's *frau*.

Glancing up, Susanna froze. Iva was back in the kitchen doorway. She obviously wasn't through talking.

"Look, *Mamm*, it's okay," Herman said, as if he knew what his mother planned to say. "I told you that before Susanna came in."

"I didn't finish what I was saying," Iva told him. "In fact, I've hardly started. I told you I wanted to wait until Susanna came in. This is something both of you need to answer."

"*Mamm!*" Herman protested. "I already know what you're going to say. Deacon Atlee settled the matter with us."

"I don't call this being settled," Iva said. "Not if Bishop Jacob is involved. And he is, you know. The poor man must have lost a *gut* year off his few remaining ones, his *frau* Mattie told me. Worrying about what Matthew told him. Thank *Da Hah* the man loves both of you or you would have been in a heap of trouble."

"It's settled," Herman repeated.

"It might be settled with Bishop Jacob, but it's not with me," Iva said. "I want to know the whole story. This kind of thing has the potential of causing an awful scandal, and I will not have my son involved. If we had known this, *Daett* and I would not have given our word to your wedding. Susanna, I want to make myself clear on that matter."

Susanna grabbed the edge of the couch for support and bit her tongue.

"Please, *Mamm*," Herman said. "Sit down and we will discuss this rationally."

"Rationally!" Iva sputtered. "What kind of big *Englisha* word is that, Herman? I never heard you using such words while you were growing up in *my* house."

"*Mamm!*" Herman exclaimed, looking quite pale.

Susanna sat down beside Herman, clutching his arm.

"You're changing." Iva wagged her finger at Herman. "Right in front of my eyes. Though if I'm honest with myself, it's been going on for some time. Soon after you started dating Susanna here. I wish we'd spoken up more. But she's your *frau* now, and nothing can be done about it."

"*Yah, Mamm,* she is," Herman said. "I don't regret marrying Susanna for one minute."

Susanna held back the sobs rising in her chest.

"And another thing," Iva continued. "I hope you're being the man of the house like you're supposed to be. All this babying can spoil a man. And let me remind you, Herman, Christmas is coming up. Already there's talk about the *Englisha* celebrations that have been taking hold in the community. And we all know that Susanna's family has been part of that, following after that *Englisha* custom of changing the day around from what *Da Hah* intended. I warned you about that when you started seeing Susanna. I'm expecting you to hold to the old ways. There are still some of us left who practice the right tradition, and I'm not having one of my family stray."

"*Yah, Mamm,*" Herman said. "I've told Susanna about Christmas."

"Thank *Da Hah* for that!" Iva turned on her heels and disappeared into the kitchen once again.

Sixteen

*A*mid the banging coming from the kitchen, Susanna saw Herman glance at her out of the corner of his eye. She didn't move because she couldn't right now. What was Herman thinking about her after his mother's tirade? He had stuck up for her, but still… Everything felt like ice, and the house had grown colder even though the registers in the floor were pouring out heat as usual.

"I'd better get the plowing done," Herman said, throwing the quilt aside.

Her mouth fell open as he rose.

"But, Herman!" She clung to his hand.

He tried to smile but failed. "I have to go. *Mamm* is correct. I should be working in the fields."

Disengaging his hand, he pulled on his boots, took his coat from a peg by the door, and then slipped it on. He opened the door and stepped outside.

Susanna ran after him. "Herman, you're sick! I can't let you go out in the fields like this. What if you have a relapse? It could be really serious then." Obviously she wasn't getting through to him because he continued walking toward the barn. Whatever his *mamm* had instilled in him as a boy was making itself known. Hard work? Determination? Shame at showing sickness? "Herman, please," she begged. "Don't do this."

He pushed open the barn door, and she followed him inside.

"Can I help then?" she asked, changing tactics.

"*Yah.*" He pointed toward the wall. "You can help me get the harnesses on the horses."

With a great heave she lifted one up and waited until he brought the Belgian out of the stall. With Herman on one end and her on the other, they threw the harness over the horse's back. Herman fastened the straps with shaking hands.

Tears stung her eyes as Susanna helped. Her man was going to work before he was over his sickness, and she clearly could do nothing about it. How could Iva do that to her child? Or worse, how could a mother do that to her son who was now a man?

With the Belgian done, Herman brought out a second horse. They repeated the process until all four horses were harnessed. Susanna led two of them outside. She had done this with her *daett* many times and knew the routine. Only *Daett* had the good sense not to work when he was deathly sick.

"Thanks," Herman said when the horses were hitched to the plow. "I'm okay now."

No you're not! she wanted to scream after him, but she pressed her lips together instead.

He bounced across the rough field, urging the horses on. For a moment he tilted sideways but caught himself just in time, righting his body in the seat.

Susanna waited until Herman reached the place he'd last been working and dropped the plow into the ground before she moved back toward the house. Whatever Iva was doing in the kitchen, Susanna didn't want to see her right now—maybe not ever. It was a wicked thought to have. Iva was Herman's *mamm.* Susanna needed to deal with this somehow. The worst problem was Iva's opinion of her. No doubt Iva believed the rumors that must even now be circulating around the community. That she and Matthew had been inappropriate in their courtship. It was so untrue, but how did one prove that?

The wash flapping on the line caught Susanna's attention, and she realized to her horror that it was already midmorning and she hadn't finished washing. The task had been forgotten in the *kafuffle* Iva had stirred up. She rushed to the basement and started the gasoline motor again, piling in another load.

The roar of the motor sounded *gut,* blocking all the sounds around her. Even the pounding anger in her heart—anger at Iva for being so stubborn and unreasonable and at Herman for listening to his *mamm* instead of her—was overtaken. Herman was a grown man and ought to know better than work while he was so sick. Keeping the traditions of his family on Christmas was one thing, but working in the fields while he was ill was entirely something else.

When the load was finished, Susanna ran the wash through the wringer. She started another batch before she left with the hamper full of damp clothes. Outside the sun had come out and was warming things up.

"Thank you, *Hah,*" she whispered, glancing toward the heavens after a long look at Herman making his rounds on the plow. "Maybe Herman won't relapse if it's warmer today."

The load of wash was soon pinned on the line, and Susanna went back to the basement for the next and final load. Hanging the last load on the line, she glanced again toward the field where Herman was busy plowing. From here he looked like he always did. Maybe he was going to be fine after all. Maybe she should stop being so dramatic. It wasn't helping anything.

With the last of the wash up, Susanna would have to face Iva. It couldn't be avoided any longer, so she headed for her kitchen where Iva was no doubt still thinking about Herman's poor choice of a *frau.* Well, the woman was who she was, and Susanna would force herself to accept her. There was little chance of changing Iva's mind about anything, but they did have to live in near proximity as family in some shape or fashion. Peacefully, she hoped. But this morning wasn't a very *gut* sign pointing in that direction.

It hurt to know that Iva wasn't happy about her son's choice of a *frau*. Maybe if she had known that, she wouldn't have married Herman. That was an awful thought, she quickly decided. If Herman would only stand up to his *mamm*. Susanna sighed. After all, Herman had stood up to his *mamm* about marrying her, and she should be happy about that.

Going up by the basement door, Susanna entered the kitchen. Iva looked like she had several cooking projects going on because flour was scattered all over the table and counter. Pie pans were set out on the counter, and bread dough was rising beside them.

"I see Herman got some sense into his head," Iva said as she looked up.

"*Yah,* I helped him harness the horses."

"I'm glad to see you also have some *gut* sense in your head. Supporting your husband like that. Maybe you do have more in you than I thought at first."

"It's *gut* you think so," Susanna managed. Antagonizing the woman would get her nowhere.

"Now, if we can get this awful rumor about you and Matthew ended, I'll feel much better." Iva pressed out the pie dough with Susanna's rolling pin.

Whatever else could be said about the woman, Susanna thought, she was efficient in the kitchen.

"What have you to say for yourself?" Iva asked.

"I take it you still think the rumor might be true? That I had things going with Matthew I shouldn't have?"

Iva shrugged. "Can't say I do or that I don't. I know your family comes with some liberal leanings, but they're okay, I suppose. That's why I consented to Herman dating you. And I knew you stayed in the community after Matthew left. Why don't you sit down and tell me the whole story?"

"There's not much to tell." She didn't want to sit down at Iva's command. Even more, she didn't want to go through the situation and feelings again. What next? Telling curious strangers on her porch her history with Matthew?

"I'd say Matthew had an awful lot to tell from the sounds of it." Iva glanced up at Susanna while she trimmed the pie dough.

Susanna found a kitchen chair with her hand and sat down.

"Do you have anything to say?" Iva stopped and looked at her.

"Nothing that will help, I suppose. I've told Herman what I have to say, and he believes me."

Iva snorted. "I'd expect that. What husband wouldn't? It's not like they wish to admit their mistakes."

"So you think I'm a mistake?"

"Now, now, I wouldn't say that. You're a pretty decent girl. And who knows whether what Matthew said is true. He's in the *bann,* after all."

"So what *did* he say?"

"Oh, I don't want to repeat it here. And it would just be hearsay anyway. I didn't hear him say it myself."

"I don't think Matthew would say something like what you're implying."

"You don't?" Iva was staring again. "You defend the man?"

"No, I'm just saying what I know about him. Matthew wouldn't lie."

"I see…" Iva continued with the pies. "An interesting way of looking at this, to say the least."

"I've told you the truth, and I can't say anything more."

"So you never were that sweet on Matthew?"

Susanna took a deep breath. "There was a time when I loved Matthew with all of my heart. He was always decent with me. But he wanted to leave the community and saw me as a weight around his neck, I suppose. Something like that. And his love wasn't big enough to get over that. So he left. But the most we ever did was kiss each other. I explained this to Herman."

Iva's face was turning red. "You don't have to tell me all the things you say to your man about love. I believe you."

"Thank you," Susanna said. And, strangely, she did feel thankful. She ought to be glad Iva hadn't run out of the house, instead of believing her after such plain talk. But how else would she have gotten through to the woman? And wouldn't that have been a funny sight? Iva running out the door with her dress flying as she fled? I must be losing my mind, Susanna thought as she choked back a laugh. Iva was looking at her again, so Susanna jumped up. "Let me help with the baking."

"I was waiting for you to offer," Iva said. "I saw you were low in bread, and there were no pies in the cupboards. Every wife ought to keep her family in pies."

"*Yah,* I know." Susanna pressed her lips together. This was a little too much. Who was Iva to lecture her on pampering her family with pies? But then Iva probably looked at the lack of pies as laziness on her part.

"I'm making cherry and blueberry," Iva was saying. "That's what you had in the cupboard. I must compliment you for at least keeping up with supplies…even if the pies weren't made."

"Maybe I should prepare lunch for Herman," Susanna suggested when she was done filling the bread pans. "While you finish the baking."

Iva nodded, continuing to work.

Clearing off a corner of the table, Susanna busied herself with making potato soup. That would be a nourishing enough meal and should be easy on a feverish stomach, she figured.

Iva raised no objections once it became obvious what Susanna was working on. She wasn't even paying her that much attention. They worked in silence, sharing the stove and the counter until Susanna finished.

Herman walked in right at twelve, looking pale and drawn. He said little while they ate and left afterward with only a muttered thanks.

Susanna wanted to run after him, to pull him back into the house and stick him in bed, but it was no use. Herman was a grown man, and she was a grown woman. They would have to deal with the world—and the people—*Da Hah* had given them.

Seventeen

The dawn was breaking as Susanna finished the chores. Herman had been tossing and turning in bed when she left the house. The whole evening and night had been awful—once Herman finally came in from the fields after his *mamm* left. His fever had been raging since supper.

She pitied him, *yah,* but she was also angry about the whole situation. The Wagler family was acting like children—all caught up in this idea of working even when they were obviously sick. And look where it got Herman—a serious setback that needed a doctor's attention.

And obviously Iva wasn't coming around this morning to look at her handiwork, either. She'd probably blame Herman for not being tough enough. The woman was enough to make Susanna scream. And she had come close to that very thing last night once Herman arrived at the barn with his team of horses.

She'd raced out to help put them up and gasped at the sight of him. "Herman! You look sick! You look like you're burning up with fever!"

He'd tried to smile. "It'll go away."

She laid her hand on his forehead. "Herman Wagler, you're sick. Really sick!"

His face showed that he knew this was the truth.

Susanna had quieted down, helping him get the horses into the barn.

"Are the chores done?" he'd asked.

"I'll do them later. You're going inside right now."

He hadn't protested as she led him toward the house. Herman had stumbled once in the lawn, and she'd shrieked, grabbing him with both hands to hold him up.

Once he was settled on the couch, she rushed to make chicken soup before running out to finish the chores. None of the food his *mamm* had made yesterday was suitable for Herman in his condition.

This morning Susanna decided that Iva was worse than useless. She was dangerous. But Susanna couldn't start thinking about that now. She had to get back inside with Herman. Dipping out a large bucket of oats, she poured it into Bruce's feedbox. He would need extra energy for the ride into Kalona this morning. Herman was going to the doctor whether he wanted to or not. Susanna was not going to lose a husband after only a few weeks of marriage—and all because of a meddling mother-in-law.

The Belgians banged in their stall at the smell of oats.

"Not today," she told them. "Herman isn't working. You can loaf around the field, but Bruce has to run into town." They neighed as Susanna let them out into the pasture. Running across the lawn, she entered the house, pausing a moment to listen. Herman had been moaning when she left, but everything was quiet now. Taking off her coat, she peeked into the bedroom. Herman had the covers thrown off his sweating body. She rushed to his side. "Herman!" she called gently.

He groaned and tried to sit up.

"You'd better stay in bed awhile longer, Herman. I'm taking you to the doctor this morning."

He pushed her hand aside and swung his legs over the edge. "What's going on? Why am I not up and dressed?"

"You're sick. And I don't care what your *mamm* says or what you're used to. You're going to see the doctor today. You're in danger of pneumonia because you've relapsed."

He groaned again, rubbing his eyes. "I had awful nightmares last night."

"I suppose you did." She ran her hand over his forehead. "You were tossing and turning most of the time."

"Did I keep you awake?"

"A little, but I'm okay."

He stared out the window at the light of dawn. "I kept hearing *Mamm* tell me to get out of bed and get into the fields. But it was cold and windy, there was snow blowing, and we couldn't get the horses out of the barn. My head hurt so much I thought it would burst. And nothing worked. The straps on the harnesses were broken, the horses' hooves were frozen to the barn floor, and they screamed in terror while we hung on to their halters. And we got nothing done. It was awful, Susanna."

"It was just a dream," Susanna comforted, laying her hand on his forehead again.

"You're here this morning," he said, as if that thought had just occurred to him. "But I'm still sick."

"It's okay." She held him tightly.

"I acted kind of foolish yesterday, didn't I?"

Yah, she wanted to say. *You certainly did.* But she held back the words. Herman knew what he'd done without her rubbing it in. But it sure was nice he was admitting it so willingly. She figured a lot of husbands would have been too stubborn.

"The doctor's visit will cost me more than the money I saved working yesterday."

Again Susanna bit her lip to hold back the words. *You could have stood up to your mamm yesterday when it would have done some* gut, *Herman.* He had stood up to his *mamm* about the rumors floating around the community though. For this she was thankful. And that was probably the reason Iva had finally believed her side of the story.

"*Mamm* didn't do us much *gut* yesterday, did she?" Herman said.

This time Susanna laughed, remembering Iva bustling around in her kitchen for most of the day. "At least your *mamm* left us plenty of baked goods."

Herman's smile grew broad. "That's *Mamm* for you. Always thinks she can make everything right by baking."

She could do much better by keeping that tongue in her mouth, Susanna almost said. Instead she said, "Your *mamm* was just trying to help."

"Next time I'm sending her the bill." Herman tried to stand, tottering on his feet for a moment before sitting down again.

"Just rest," she told him. "I'll get you something to eat, and then we can head out to the doctor."

"There's got to be some way not to visit the doctor. He's too expensive."

Susanna ignored the comment. "Do you think you can keep oatmeal down?"

He nodded, saying nothing more about the doctor visit, and slid back under the covers

Tucking him under the quilt again, Susanna left for the kitchen. The water soon boiled, and she pushed one of Iva's pies aside to make room for the oatmeal bowl.

She ought to feed Herman pie this morning so he could see for himself what his *mamm* had spent her day doing while he was getting sicker by the minute in the field. But that would be mean and serve no purpose. Plus, she would feel bad making Herman eat pie when he had a fever and needed nutritious food.

With the oatmeal done, she carried the steaming bowl to the bedroom.

Herman smiled when she entered and pulled himself to a sitting position.

She spoon-fed him, and he didn't object.

"I think I'm well enough now that I don't need to see the doctor," he said, when the bowl was empty.

"You're seeing the doctor, Herman. The office opens at eight, and if we get there early we won't have to wait that long."

He groaned but looked resigned when she smiled at him.

"I'll eat some breakfast, and then we'll be on our way."

He slid back down in bed and pulled the quilt up to his chin.

Hurrying into the kitchen, Susanna prepared her own breakfast, sliding a piece of pie on a plate. Berry pie wasn't exactly something that went with oatmeal, but Iva's efforts shouldn't go to waste. Susanna smiled at the thought. She was obviously a daughter-in-law Iva hadn't anticipated having. Someone who took her son Herman out of the safe waters of the family harbor. Iva probably wished Herman had chosen someone like Millie Troyer for a *frau*. Millie was so meek she hardly spoke unless spoken to. And Herman could have gotten to Millie in time—if he'd wanted to. Millie hadn't dated Jesse Byler until after Herman had taken Susanna home for the first time. Millie would certainly not have stood up to Iva…or wanted her family to have *Englisha* Christmas customs.

Placing the dirty dishes on the counter, Susanna hurried back to the bedroom. She changed into a better dress and helped Herman get his Sunday pants and shirt on. He moaned most of the time but didn't protest about going anymore.

With Herman ensconced on the couch, she dashed to the barn to bring Bruce out and hitch him to the buggy. When she was done, she left the horse tied to the hitching post, found an extra buggy blanket near the grain bin and threw it on the buggy seat, and then went in to get Herman.

She dressed him in two coats and pulled his wool hat on his head. He almost looked like he was enjoying the fussing. She kissed him on the cheek and he smiled. Herman followed her, and she held the front door open for him. In the yard she held his arm, but he seemed steady enough on his feet. He even climbed into the buggy by himself. Unsnapping Bruce's tie rope, she threw it under the seat and joined Herman, making sure he had both buggy blankets tightly wound around him.

"Let's go!" she hollered to Bruce after she lifted the reins.

Bruce lumbered down the driveway.

Driving past Bishop Jacob's place, there was no sign of anyone around. *They must not be working outside today.* Susanna noted the field beside the barn showed fresh signs of plowing, probably done yesterday.

"They're done," Herman muttered.

"I'm sorry," Susanna said, glancing at him. "You'll get your work done yet. Much faster than if you get pneumonia."

He coughed for the first time this morning and turned away to cough more.

Alarm flashed across her face.

Turning back, he looked at her. "I'm okay."

"After you have antibiotics in you, you'll be okay."

"I agree," he said. "*Mamm* isn't right about everything."

What a relief! she wanted to shout, but she didn't.

"Maybe she's also wrong about something else."

"*Yah?*" Susanna said absently, gently slapping the reins against Bruce's back to hurry him along.

"About Christmas with your family. I've seen how they were at Thanksgiving. They just enjoyed the day and were truly thankful to *Da Hah.*"

Susanna took a deep breath. What was Herman saying? Iva had made it clear how much her family's practice of Christmas was forbidden by the Waglers.

"I've been thinking about this matter. Well, just overnight really. And yesterday out plowing in the field while feeling like I did. You're so different from what I'm used to."

"I suppose I am," Susanna managed to say. "I'm working on accepting your family's ways. And I'm falling in love with you more every day." She smiled at him.

Herman didn't say anything for a while.

"It's true!" Susanna glanced at him with a sweet smile. "I think you're quite a man."

"I don't know about that," he murmured. "You got a *gut* look at *Mamm* yesterday. And I'm sure the sight wasn't all that pretty."

"She's your *mamm,* Herman. I won't say anything ill of her."

"You just take me to the doctor and mother me once she's gone, is that it?"

"I'm not planning to be like her. I'm your *frau*—not your mother."

He was silent again, and she gave him more of the buggy blankets as they drove through the edge of town. He shivered but shook his head when a worried look flashed across her face again. "I'm okay," he repeated. "And I'm also thinking how wonderful a *frau* you make for me. It's so different, and so…" He let the words hang.

"Well, I'm glad you approve." Susanna squeezed his arm under the blankets.

"Susanna, we're going to Christmas at your *mamm* and *daett's* place this year."

"Now I know your head is touched with the fever!" she exclaimed. And it was true. She wouldn't hold him to something he said while he was obviously delirious.

"I'm perfectly whole," he defended, seeing the look on her face. He pulled the blankets tighter.

"Here we are!" she said, stopping in front of the clinic. "Now let's get you inside and fixed up before you get worse."

He groaned as he climbed down after she'd tied Bruce to a tree.

All Susanna could think of was the tongue lashing or worse Iva would give the both of them if she ever heard what Herman had just said. Well, her lips were sealed. She'd never tell.

Eighteen

Susanna stood at the living room window and looked out over the open fields. This was almost too *gut* to be true. And yet there it was, right in front of her eyes. Bishop Jacob and his son-in-law, both with teams of Belgians, were helping Herman with the plowing. They lined up at the end of the field and began, each slightly behind and to the side of the other as black dirt spilled from under the plow blades.

Herman was better this morning. He'd rested all last week and even stayed home from Sunday services again. That must have been what caused the outpouring of concern this morning. Herman's continued absence—and she'd even stayed home on Sunday to be with him. She wasn't going alone, she'd told Herman. Not this Sunday.

The doctor had been adamant that Herman rest for the remainder of the week while the antibiotics did their work. He said dire consequences could result if Herman worked. Herman had groaned but listened. He stomped around the house as the end of the week moved closer and he was feeling better, but he stayed inside. Susanna had done the best she could to keep him occupied, but it wasn't like Herman could do housework. And eating only lasted so long.

His *mamm's* pies were all gone. Susanna smiled. Iva's work had saved her from having to bake last week, which had given her time to clean the house thoroughly. Why she did it, she wasn't sure. But Christmastime was approaching, and she wanted a clean house even though it would be only Herman and her here on Christmas morning.

Wouldn't it be wonderful, she thought, if Herman really meant what he'd said about celebrating Christmas with her family? How perfect such a day would be. But it was completely out of the question. Herman had been affected by the fever on the way to the doctor's office. He'd said nothing more about celebrating Christmas since then. And she wasn't going to bring it up. A fuss would only spoil the joy that was growing between them. Yet the thought of the Christmas celebration wouldn't go away. It kept coming back during the long evenings, especially the past week as they sat and drank hot chocolate.

She'd finally decided that celebrating Christmas in a certain way was really only a silly notion. Sure, it would be absolutely *wunderbah* to spend the day like her family did, but there were other *gut* ways to spend the time too. And she and Herman would find them. Just like they were finding more and more love for each other. Herman couldn't get enough of her kisses, now that he was feeling better. And she couldn't get enough of his strong arms wrapped around her. This love was a great gift from *Da Hah,* and something for which they both gave much thanks.

In the meantime, Susanna had better stop staring out of the window and get busy with her Monday-morning wash. If Bishop Jacob and his son-in-law came over to help Herman out of concern, then perhaps someone else would also be along soon—if she didn't miss her guess. Herman's *mamm* would have a hard time staying away since her son had missed another church service.

Iva would stop in to give Herman a *gut* lecture, if nothing else. But it wouldn't do any *gut*. Susanna had doctor's orders that backed her stand of making Herman rest all week. She held back a giggle. Maybe she'd get another batch of pies out of the deal. The bread pantry was still well stocked from the bread Iva had baked last week. So she would get to tell Iva—if she showed up—no more bread.

At least I have an interesting mother-in-law, Susanna thought as she went into the bedroom to gather up their dirty clothing. Herman hadn't used quite as many pants and shirts last week, so maybe two batches of wash were all she had to hang out. Iva would think they'd been wearing the same clothes all week, which was partly true. At least Herman had because he wasn't working.

Iva could think what she wanted. Before long there might be a *bobbli* on the way! Not that she showed any signs yet, but hopefully it would happen. And likely many more after that. Then there would be plenty of wash on the line for Iva to see.

Susanna took the hamper into the basement and started the gas motor on the second pull. I'm getting *gut* with this motor, she thought. The one at home had its own quirks, just like this one did. Here you had to pull the choke halfway out instead of all the way like she used to with *mamm* and *daett's* motor.

With the roar of the motor in her ear, Susanna laughed. Herman wasn't quite like a motor, but she was getting to know his little quirks too. Let his *mamm* think what she wished, but Herman had blossomed under her care. The doctor's antibiotics had helped, but so had her doting.

And she was *gut* at it. What a *wunderbah* feeling. This was something she'd never felt with Matthew. Doting on Matthew was hard to imagine. Herman seemed to grow stronger by it. She could feel it in how he held her in the evenings and in the strength of his smile. Herman's *mamm* might think spoiling a man made him weak, but it wasn't true in Herman's case. Susanna's loving care made him stronger. She had plenty of proof of that.

Susanna finished running the first load through the wringer and started the next before going outside. She was hanging the last piece on the line when Iva came driving down the lane. Susanna started toward the barn to help her unhitch, and then she stopped. Last time Iva made her do all of the work, so this time it was Iva's turn. Yet Iva was Herman's *mamm*…but a person could only take so much. And with all the lectures she'd received from Iva's sharp tongue about Herman being babied last week, it might be best to postpone such moments. At least until she could gather herself together to face the onslaught.

Without looking at Iva parked beside the barn, Susanna turned and marched to the basement. A quick glance at the last moment showed Iva staring after her, mouth dropped open, probably from shock. Susanna suppressed a giggle and quickly closed the basement door behind her. It really wasn't funny, but Iva was only getting her own medicine. Susanna would deal with the consequences later.

Susanna's heart sank when she came back out with the last load of wash. Herman was standing beside the now-unhitched buggy, in deep conversation with his *mamm*. Behind him his team of Belgians stood alongside the fencerow waiting for him. Bishop Jacob and his son-in-law were still plowing.

Obviously Herman had stopped his work to help his *mamm* with her horse. Maybe she should rush over and apologize, Susanna thought. But no matter. Iva would have plenty to say to her later.

Sure enough, she wasn't even done hanging the last piece of wash before Iva marched over.

"*Gut* morning," Susanna said, trying to sound sweet.

"Don't you believe in making your kinfolk welcome around here?" Iva demanded, skipping the morning's greeting. "At least my son has the decency to come help his poor mother unhitch her horse. My poor bones ache enough in the morning without having to do all the work myself."

"I'm sorry," Susanna said. And she did feel just a little sorry, now that she thought about Iva's arthritis. "Is it very bad?"

"Ach," Iva said, "it comes and goes, and one shouldn't complain. Do you need help with the next load of wash?"

"I'm done," Susanna said.

"This is all the wash you have? What was Herman doing all last week?"

"He was in bed," Susanna said, "by doctor's orders. He got a pretty bad setback from being out all day with a fever. You know… the last time you were here."

"Well, it was *gut* to see him working that day," Iva said, obviously not very repentant. "At least Bishop Jacob and his son-in-law are out this morning helping. It was getting way late in the year for fall plowing, and with an early winter threatening. We can be very thankful to *Da Hah* for the *wunderbah* help the community is to each other."

"*Yah*," Susanna agreed, "this is true."

Behind Iva, Susanna saw Herman walking toward them. She hadn't noticed he was still around. What did Herman have to say that was so important it couldn't wait until lunchtime?

Herman cleared his throat, and Iva whirled around. "Now don't you go sneaking up on me like that. I'm too old a woman for such sudden starts."

"Sorry, *Mamm*," Herman said. "I didn't mean to startle you."

Iva nodded and launched into another flow of words. "Don't you think you should be out in the fields working? I mean, I appreciate the help with the horse since Susanna was so busy." Iva paused to glare at Susanna. "But one must not take advantage of free help the community gives. There's still an hour or so before lunch. And I told you I brought along plenty of potato soup for everyone. So you don't have to worry about Susanna not having enough food for Bishop Jacob and his son-in-law."

Susanna wanted to scream at this barb—and likely would have if Herman hadn't spoken up first.

"Susanna is perfectly capable of making lunch, *Mamm*. I wasn't worried about that. What I wanted to tell you is something that shouldn't be said at lunch in front of Bishop Jacob."

"What has happened now?" Iva demanded.

Susanna held her breath as Herman continued. "Nothing, *Mamm*. It's what is going to happen."

Iva glared at him. "Like what, Herman?"

He didn't seem troubled by his *mamm's* baleful gaze. He continued in an even voice. "See, *Mamm*, it's like this. Susanna and I are going to spend Christmas morning with her *mamm* and *daett* and their family, wherever the gathering is held. This tradition is something that means a lot to Susanna, and I want to make it a part of our new family."

Susanna stared at Herman openmouthed and then she shrieked. She just couldn't help it.

Iva ignored the outburst. "What has gotten into you, Herman? You cannot do this! We have our own tradition."

"It's a *gut* tradition for our family, *Mamm*," Herman said. "But Susanna and I are a new family now, and we'll establish our own tradition."

"I have never heard anything like this!" Iva turned to Susanna. "Did you put him up to this? By charming and babying him? I do declare, a man's heart can be turned so easily."

Susanna worked her mouth, but no sound came out. What could she say to such a charge?

"*Mamm*, this is my decision, so you might as well accept it," Herman said. "The less fuss the better."

"Well!" Iva said as Herman turned on his heels and went back to his team.

"I...I had...really, I didn't...it was nothing I did." Susanna searched for more words after Iva turned her gaze back to her.

"Like I'm going to believe that," Iva huffed. She muttered something Susanna couldn't quite hear and then, after a moment's silence, said, "Well, why are we standing out here in the cold cackling like a couple of old hens? My soup is getting cold in the buggy, and we have to get dinner ready. I wasn't expecting extra people here, but thank *Da Hah* I followed His inspiration and made plenty."

"*Yah,* that was *gut,*" Susanna managed as she followed Iva to the buggy.

A hamper dangling from one arm, Susanna helped Iva carry the large kettle of soup with the other. It was a lot of soup from the looks of things. Plenty for lunch and for the rest of the week.

Susanna almost shrieked again, remembering what Herman had said. They were going home for Christmas! Nothing Iva said today could take that joy away.

erman had the buggy ready when Susanna dashed out of the house. Bruce looked at her and whinnied like he knew how happy she was.

"You dear thing," she said, stopping to pat him on the neck.

"What about me?" Herman asked, peering around Bruce's head. "Don't I at least get a goodbye kiss?"

"You'll get more than that!" Susanna said, throwing her arms around him.

"This is public," he warned with a smile. "What if the bishop and his daughter happen to drive by?"

"Then they will see how much I love you!" Susanna let go, patting her husband on the cheek. "There now, you don't have to blush like a girl."

"I'm not blushing," he said, growing even redder.

She laughed and gave him another hug. "Thanks so much for this. I promise I'll be back in plenty of time to fix supper. There's a sandwich ready for your lunch. I'll even come home early enough to help with the chores."

"You don't have to," he protested. "With the plowing done, I'm caught up with the farm work. When you get back, I'll relax and enjoy life with you. And, of course, Christmas is coming…"

"Oh Herman! You don't know how much this means to me. I know I'm being silly and all, but that's just the way I am."

"I like the way you are!" He took her hand and led her up to the buggy steps. "Off you go! Tell Mary hello for me."

She climbed into the buggy and picked up the reins. "I'll do that!" She waved as Bruce dashed forward, apparently catching some of the Christmas spirit himself. Down the road Susanna noticed their *Englisha* neighbor's Christmas tree was twinkling in the front window.

I need to calm down, Susanna thought. She settled Bruce into a steady clip on the road. Her pent-up excitement was to blame. All those days of trying to give up hope of ever spending Christmas with her family again. Only to have Herman make such a turnaround!

Susanna held the reins tightly as they drove past Bishop Jacob's place. The bishop's son-in-law was walking from the house to the barn. She waved and he waved back, a perplexed look on his face. No doubt he wondered why Bruce was lifting his feet so high in the air and she was smiling so big this morning. If he only knew! But he probably didn't think Christmas was a big deal either.

Susanna laughed out loud. Iva was the one who had pushed Herman over the edge. She was the one to thank for the Christmas celebration this year. But Susanna would never mention that to Iva. The simple fact was that Herman had been given a *gut* look at the old and at the new. And he had chosen her way over whatever attachment he used to have for his *mamm's* way.

Herman was now twice the man he had been before, regardless of what Iva thought about the matter. Iva was probably worried about the danger of Herman going liberal, which wasn't going to happen. And she was no doubt mourning her loss of ability to boss Herman around. Oh, she would surely still try, but Herman had shown he could—and would—stand up to her. For that alone, Susanna could hug and kiss him all over again if he were in the buggy with her.

Herman would be with her on Christmas morning, celebrating

at *Mamm* and *Daett's* place. That's where the family had decided to hold the gathering this year. Herman would be a little nervous probably, this being his first Christmas celebration, but he'd be okay.

Susanna remembered with a smile how Mary had taken her aside last Sunday, a pained expression on her face. She'd whispered into her ear, "I'm making candies next week. Do you think Herman would at least let you come for that? It doesn't mean you'd have to be with us for Christmas morning."

Susanna had quickly hidden her smile, just as she'd been hiding Herman's change of mind from her family. After all, what if Herman changed his mind again? Or if Iva came up with a hard-hitting argument to influence him? But neither had happened. Iva had made no further attempts to persuade Herman. It was as if she knew when she was defeated so she withdrew gracefully. That was a nice characteristic to have in a mother-in-law, Susanna figured.

Iva's eyes even seemed to have a tiny bit of admiration in them for her now. As if Iva held her victorious rival in higher esteem. Susanna hadn't been trying to compete with Iva. She just wanted be a *gut frau* for Herman.

"I have to tell you something," Susanna had whispered back to Mary last Sunday. "Herman and I are coming to Christmas breakfast at *Mamm* and *Daett's!*"

Mary's eyes had gotten big. "How did you manage that?"

"I didn't manage anything," Susanna said, but Mary didn't look convinced.

"Wow, I need to learn your secrets and practice them on Ernest."

"You'll do no such thing!" Susanna had whispered back. "I didn't do anything. It was *Da Hah!*"

Mary shrugged. "I'm sure He helped."

Da Hah had done more than help, Susanna told herself. He had done all of it...even getting Iva to help.

Up ahead a parked *Englisha* car along the road caught her attention. Susanna slowed down, preparing to go around. She noticed a woman walking below the branches of a small tree with scissors in her hand, snipping busily away.

As Susanna came closer, she realized what the lady was doing. She was working on a bush full of red berries. An idea gripped her. There were enough berries on that tree for her and the *Englisha* woman. Why shouldn't she stop?

"Whoa," she called out to Bruce. He came to a halt behind the *Englisha* car.

"There's plenty here for everyone!" the *Englisha* woman sang out when she noticed Susanna.

Susanna climbed out of the buggy. "Don't be running off," she told Bruce, patting his neck as she walked past.

"Hello, I'm Constance," the woman said, giving Susanna a cheery smile. "Like I said, there's plenty here. And it doesn't seem to be anyone's private property. I think it's all right."

"*Gut* morning," Susanna greeted her. "I'm sure it's all right. My name is Susanna, and I only need a few branches."

"Help yourself." Constance waved toward the other side of the tree.

"They're so pretty," Susanna said, trying to break off a small branch brimming with red berries.

"Here, you can borrow my scissors," Constance said. "I have to run what I've cut off to the car anyway."

"Thank you." Susanna took the scissors and clipped away while Constance left. A small cedar tree grew beside the bush. It had the most delicate green branches. Clipping a few of those too, Susanna had gathered a small pile of berries and branches by the time Constance came back.

"That's all you need?" Constance asked. "I'm trying to get enough to decorate my whole kitchen."

"It's enough," Susanna said, feeling a blush creeping up her neck. "I won't need that much. Thank you so much for the use of your scissors." She handed them back to the *Englisha* woman.

"You're more than welcome," Constance said.

Susanna picked up her pile and made her way back to the buggy. Bruce looked at the greenery in her arms as if he wanted a bite.

"No way!" she said. "This is for something other than eating. You have oats at home."

Placing her cedar branches and red berries in the back of the buggy, Susanna climbed into the vehicle and slapped the lines against the horse's back. Bruce pulled out and set off at his steady pace. When she arrived at Mary's place, no one was around. Susanna pulled up next to the barn, unhitched, and led Bruce inside.

A shiver ran through her at the memory of Matthew's car parked behind the barn on Thanksgiving Day. That seemed a long time ago now, like it was from another world. She had only *Da Hah* to thank that Matthew hadn't done real damage with his loose mouth. It was hard to imagine he meant harm, but Matthew was such an easy talker.

Susanna took the branches and berries out for a few minutes to look at them. A smile crossed her face. These were exactly what she needed. And she wouldn't tell Herman anything about them until Christmas Day. This would be a little surprise for him. The project was a little silly, perhaps, but she wanted to give him something really special.

Twisting the branches into each other, she paused to hold them at arm's length. It would work—even better than she'd first thought. And the berries made a perfect offset for the green cedar. Leaving everything behind the seat, Susanna walked briskly to the house. She'd been dawdling all morning. First with Herman and then with cutting the berry and cedar branches. Mary was probably already well into the candy making, and she had still not shown her face.

Bursting into the house without knocking, Susanna hollered out, "*Gut* morning!"

Mose and Laura peeked out from the kitchen door with broad grins. Laura had little smudges of flour on her cheeks.

"We're out here!" Mary called. "Deep into candy making."

"That's what I thought." Susanna went into the kitchen. "And here I've been taking forever to get here."

"I'm sure you weren't wasting your time." Mary looked like she knew more than she did.

"I *was* a little detained," Susanna allowed.

Mary laughed. "We have all day. It's okay."

"I can't get back home too late," Susanna said.

"I understand. You're probably being extra nice to Herman these days because you're coming to Christmas breakfast."

It's not like that at all, Susanna wanted to say. But Mary wouldn't believe her, and further explanation would take much too long. She'd leave well enough alone. "I stopped along the road to cut some cedar and berry branches. I want to make something special for Herman for Christmas," she said instead.

"That's the way to do it," Mary said. "Now get out of the kitchen, children. Susanna and I have to work really hard. And you'll just be tempted to eat the dough before it's ready."

"But we want candy!" Laura protested.

"You'll get plenty," Mary told her. "Once the candies are done."

Laura puckered her face but she disappeared into the living room. Mose was already halfway out the washroom door, headed for the barn.

"Candy, candy," Mary said. "The children are just like husbands."

"I know!" Susanna said with a laugh.

"Well, your Herman deserves it. You can be thankful Matthew's little trick didn't work over Thanksgiving," Mary said. "I know he's my husband's brother, but it was very wrong what he tried to do."

"What?" Susanna let the question hang.

"Well, Deacon Atlee was over to your place. I know that much."

"Deacon Atlee believed me when I said nothing inappropriate

had gone on between Matthew and me, as did Herman. I can't believe Matthew would deliberately lie."

Mary shrugged. "I doubt if he did. Bishop Jacob isn't saying what he told him. Ernest heard Matthew blabbing in the barn around some of the older boys. You know, about making things right that he did wrong during his dating years. It could have been construed wrong, I'm sure."

"I'm just glad Herman believed me."

"Do you know who your biggest supporter is right now?"

"Herman, of course." Susanna didn't hesitate.

"Maybe," Mary allowed. "But it's also his *mamm*. Iva sticks up for you at the drop of a hat. I guess that's normal."

It is anything *but* normal, Susanna thought. But she wasn't going to say so. That would take more explanation.

"I think Matthew was trying to win you over again," Mary said. "Not that I have any proof. I'm just guessing."

"But I'm married."

"He didn't know that when he first came. And he lives in a different world, you know."

"I think Matthew was only trying to do what he said he was doing," Susanna said. "Finding healing for his past. Just like we all are. That and growing ever closer to his family and *Da Hah*."

"I suppose that's a *gut* attitude to have about the man," Mary said, carrying a pan over to the counter. "Look there—it's snowing outside."

Susanna moved to the window. Outside, fluffy white flakes were drifting past, seeming to hang in the air for long moments. Little Mose was racing around in the yard chasing them, his hands outstretched.

"It's so beautiful," Susanna said. "So very beautiful."

"*Yah,* it is," Mary agreed, walking toward the washroom door. "And it looks like I'd better get a cap for Mose's head before he catches a cold."

Twenty

*B*ruce neighed as Herman turned into the lane of Susanna's *mamm* and *daett's* house on Christmas morning.

"He knows he's coming to a familiar and comfortable place," Susanna whispered, hanging onto Herman's arm under the buggy blanket.

Herman laughed. "He just smelled the other horses in the barn. And what is this? All of your family is already here?"

"I told you they get out early," Susanna said, throwing off the blanket as Herman pulled to a stop beside the other buggies.

No one was in sight as they climbed out.

"Where is everybody?" Herman asked.

"Probably inside with the children opening presents."

Herman stopped short. "You give presents on Christmas?"

"Just to the children, and they aren't wrapped up like the *Englisha* do so it's not the same."

"Oh…" Herman unhitched Bruce.

"It'll be okay. You won't regret coming with me."

"I know I won't." Herman offered a smile. "I get to see you all day."

"Now you're being silly," she said, holding the shafts as he moved Bruce.

"But you like it when I'm silly." He paused with his hand on Bruce's bridle to glance at Susanna.

"You're not getting any more kisses!" she said. "Especially out here where everyone can see us if they just look out the window. Now get moving!"

He laughed as he disappeared into the barn with their horse.

Susanna waited until Herman returned. They held hands on the way up the walk. *Daett* had shoveled the snow and spread salt, but Susanna still clung to Herman. He was being so *wunderbah* this morning she could hardly catch her breath.

The front door burst open before they arrived, and Mary rushed out to give Susanna a hug. "I'm so glad you could make it! I kept having nightmares you'd change your mind at the last minute."

"We wouldn't do anything like that," Herman protested, feigning that his feelings had been injured.

Mary glanced at him with a worried look.

"He's as sweet as pecan pie," Susanna said. "Now don't you worry."

A smile spread across Mary's face. "Thanks for coming, Herman. I hope you enjoy our little celebration."

"I'm sure I will," Herman said with a smile.

"Come!" Susanna pulled on Herman's hand. Mary held the door as they stepped inside, where the noise level was much higher. Children were playing in the living room, setting up homemade painted blocks in one corner and driving miniature wooden horses pulling farm implements in the center. Several girls sat on the couch holding dolls, and homemade dollhouses of various sizes were on the floor in front of them.

"Who makes all this stuff?" Herman asked.

"The parents," Susanna replied.

"You didn't tell me about this."

"I didn't want to scare you off. We won't have to make anything until we have children." Susanna squeezed his hand.

"I'll look forward to that!" he said.

Susanna held still, letting her gaze take in the whole scene for a moment. Children playing. Uncles and aunts standing in the background watching. *Daett* and *Mamm* sitting on their rockers. They were so into the moment of this joy that they hardly noticed them. Was this not what coming home meant?

Then *Daett* looked up and leaped to his feet. "I thought I heard the door open, but I'm hard of hearing with all this noise going on. Well, well, if it isn't Herman and Susanna. Welcome, welcome!"

Susanna tried to keep from crying as *Daett* shook Herman's hand. He motioned for them to join the others. They did, with Herman leading the way around the circle to shake everyone's hand.

"I heard you had a bout with the flu," Ernest said, when they ended up standing beside him. "Pretty rough time, huh?"

"*Yah,*" Herman admitted. "Susanna took good care of me."

Susanna could only smile. Who would have thought things would end up this way? She had prayed for true love to grow in her heart for her husband instead of just wanting Herman to give her what she wanted. And now she had both. It was almost too much. If she didn't stop thinking this way soon, she would be crying for sure.

Thankfully it looked like *Mamm* was ready for breakfast to be announced. Sure enough, *Daett* came out of the kitchen and waved his hand. "Okay, everybody! Time to eat. *Mamm* says the food is *gut* and ready."

Susanna followed Herman into the huge dining room where the table was set up. Food would soon be spread on the table. All the things she had seen so often during her growing-up years: ham, bacon, eggs, pancakes, and golden maple syrup made from their own trees. A simple enough meal, but this was home, and it meant so much more than she could explain—even to Herman.

When they were seated, Herman squeezed her hand under the table and they exchanged glances. Somehow he had come to understand. He had seen much more of her heart in these last weeks than she'd realized. Leaning against his shoulder, she let a

few tears run down her cheeks. No one would notice, she decided.
She didn't wipe them away.

"Everyone, please be quiet for a moment," Daett said from his
place at the head of the table. "We're so happy that everyone could
come. The entire family is here this morning! This doesn't always
happen for various reasons, but we are glad *Da Hah* allowed it
today. Now, if *Mamm* will bring me the Bible, I will read the story
of why we are celebrating."

Mamm jumped up and disappeared into the living room. She
quickly returned carrying a huge German Bible.

Daett opened it to the correct page and began reading the words
Susanna had heard so many times before. They were like music this
morning, divine music playing in the air, as if the angels were here
singing just for them.

Daett read on, relating the story of a young couple who could
find no place to stay for the night. Of a young mother who carried
heaven's Child in her womb. Who had found a man who believed
in her honor. Susanna held on to Herman's hand under the table.
She was no Mary, but she'd felt a little bit of what Mary must have
gone through. What horrible things people must have said about
her when they discovered she was pregnant before marrying Joseph.

When the story came to the baby being born in the manger,
even the children were listening, just as Susanna had during her
childhood. What precious seeds were being planted in their young
minds, she thought. Just as they had been planted in hers. Oh that
these seeds will also grow into a great crop! One day these children
could also love their own spouses and gather around a family table
like this. She briefly thought about what it would be like to be sitting at home if Herman hadn't changed his mind...or if Iva hadn't
changed it for him.

Herman must have noticed her tears forming because he smiled
down at her.

Susanna turned her attention back to the story, seeing the

angels in her mind as they filled the heavens with their song of joy. A smile played on her face.

"That is a *gut* and precious story," *Daett* said when he finished. He closed the Bible and handed it back to *Mamm*, who scurried off to return it to its place in the living room.

"And now for our song," *Daett* said. "Perhaps Susanna can start it for us this morning. I can't remember exactly who led out last year, but I suppose it doesn't matter."

"*Yah*, it's Susanna's turn," one of her sisters agreed.

Susanna choked. She could hardly talk at the moment, let alone sing.

"I would love to hear Susanna sing this morning," *Daett* said. And that settled it.

Susanna took a deep breath and began singing in a trembling voice. The others joined in with the familiar melody of *Silent Night*. The room rang with the German words sang from memory: *"Stille Nacht, heilige Nacht, alles schläft; einsam wacht."*

When the last note of the last verse had been sung, *Daett* said, "Let us pray." He led out in a steady voice, "Our Father which art in heaven, hallowed be thy name…"

When the prayer ended, several of the sisters jumped up and moved quickly into the kitchen. They returned with the steaming food, which was passed around the table. When the first food dish came to Herman, he held the platter for Susanna and said, "Take some first."

"*Nee*," she objected. "I ought to hold it for you."

He gave her a stern look, and Susanna gave in and filled her plate. Only then did he help himself and pass the food on.

"Thank you," she whispered. He was being so nice. Pretty soon she'd be crying again.

"You're welcome," he whispered back. "And thanks for bringing me here."

Now she was surely going to cry! Susanna laid her fork down to dab her moist eyes with her napkin. Across the table Mary smiled at her. Susanna managed a smile back.

"It's turning out to be a very *wunderbah* day," Mary leaned across the table to say.

Susanna didn't trust her voice, but thankfully Herman answered for both of them. "*Yah,* it is. I'm very blessed to be here."

"We're blessed to have you," Mary said, and Ernest, sitting beside her, nodded.

The meal continued with happy chatter rising and falling for close to an hour. After *Daett*'s closing prayer of thanks, the children rushed back to their new toys. Most of the older boys went outside to play in the snow and had soon erected a sizable snow fort.

Susanna helped clear the table, joining in the talk to catch up on the news with her sisters and *mamm*. The men settled in the living room. The womenfolk soon drifted to that room too, and Susanna sat next to Herman and nestled in close. Most of the other couples were doing the same. Ernest and Mary were leaning against a wall while sitting on a blanket, warming themselves in front of the woodstove.

Candy and goodies were brought out and spread on the table, along with finger foods. A steady stream of people moved past the holiday fare whenever they wished, filling plates and settling down to munch away.

By late afternoon the buggies began leaving, most of them full of children leaning out to wave as they drove down the lane. Susanna waited beside their buggy while Herman brought Bruce out of the barn. She climbed in after the tugs were fastened on her side. When Herman was settled in, she tucked the buggy blanket around both of them as they took off. Neither of them said much until they pulled into their own driveway and had Bruce comfortably munching oats in the barn.

"Come," Susanna said, taking Herman's hand to lead him behind the buggy.

"What is this all about?" he asked.

"Just wait," she said mysteriously. She reached behind a hay bale and pulled out a small bag she'd hidden.

Herman watched closely as Susanna took out a wreath of cedar branches and colorful red berries.

"Your Christmas gift. From my heart to yours. Thank you so much for everything."

"Is this like…like what you gave to…to…to him?" Herman held the wreath and looked at Susanna.

"*Nee*," Susanna said. "This is much nicer—and made just for you."

Herman took the wreath and held it up, inspecting it. "It's beautiful! I will treasure it always." Then he bent over and kissed her. "Merry Christmas," Herman said as he released her. "Isn't that what the *Englisha* say?"

"*Yah,*" she said. "They do."

Jerry Eicher books offered by Harvest House Publishers

The Adams County Trilogy

Rebecca's Promise

Rebecca's Return

Rebecca's Choice

Hannah's Heart

A Dream for Hannah

A Hope for Hannah

A Baby for Hannah

Little Valley Series

A Wedding Quilt for Ella

Ella's Wish

Ella Finds Love Again

Fields of Home Series

Missing Your Smile

Following Your Heart

Where Love Grows

Stand-alone Books

The Amish Family Cookbook

My Dearest Naomi

Susanna's Christmas Wish

*F*rom the home of bestselling author Jerry Eicher (more than 400,000 books sold) and his wife, Tina, comes this warm and inviting peek into an Amish kitchen, complete with…

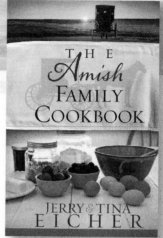

AMISH RECIPES

Hannah Byler's Pecan Pie

Beat on low speed slightly or with hand beater:
3 eggs, 1/3 cup butter, melted, 1 cup light corn syrup
½ t. salt, 2/3 cup sugar
Stir in: 1 cup pecan halves.
Pour into: 1 pie crust.
Bake at 375° for 40-50 minutes.

AMISH PROVERBS

It takes seven to cook for to make a really happy wife.

AMISH HUMOR

The *Englisha* visitor suffered through a three-hour Amish wedding service, sitting on the hard, backless church bench.

"Why does it take so long to tie the knot?" he asked afterward.

"Well," the bishop said, stroking his long, white beard. "So that it takes 'em a lifetime to untie it."

 Readers will laugh, pray, and eat robustly with *The Amish Family Cookbook* at their side.